TWO COWBOYS ONE BRIDE

LACEY DAVIS

VIRTUAL BOOKSELLER

Copyright

Copyright © 2021 Lacey Davis
Published by Virtual Bookseller, LLC
All Rights Reserved
Cover Art by Dar Albert
Edited by Tina Winograd
Release date: February 2021
ebook ISBN 978-1-950858-43-9
Paperback ISBN 978-1-950858-51-4

This book and parts thereof may not be reproduced in any form, stored in a retrieval system, or transmitted in any form by any means—electronic, mechanical, photocopying, or otherwise—without prior written permission of the author and publisher, except as provided by the United States of America copyright law. The only exception is by a reviewer who may quote short excerpts in a review.

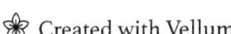 Created with Vellum

A Runaway Bride...Two Texas Rangers

Heiress Belle Walker will be wed within the hour. But after overhearing her fiancé's plans for their "life" together, she must run or soon be six feet under. Another victim of Lester Clark's "accidents." She never thought her escape would put her in the path of two Texas Rangers.

Jackson Moore and Cal Thomas rescue Belle lost and wandering on the prairie in a wedding gown. Miles from town, this runaway bride needs their help.

The twist—they didn't expect her to heal their hearts. Could she be the woman they've longed for all these years, who will settle down between them or will her ex-fiancé destroy the life they're trying to create?

Sign up for my New Book Alert and receive a free book — Blindfold Me.

https://www.subscribepage.com/laceydavis_author

1

On a hot August day, Bella Walker sat inside a room in the back of the church. A place brides had waited for years. Today was her wedding day. Uneasiness gripped her as she waited for the ceremony to begin. The chapel was filled with people from town and she heard the whispers regarding her marriage.

Even she had misgivings.

No, she wasn't in love, but no other man had courted her. No one seemed to want her and she was nearing the old maid age of twenty-one. She longed for a home and family, children, and a man to love and care for her.

Was Lester Clark the man to give her what she desired? Share his bed and bear his children?

A sigh escaped her as she thought of her own parents. They had a love match. And when one died, the other one went soon after.

An only child, they had left her wealthy and alone when they passed from this world to the next. She had a modest home in town where she could comfortably live her life, but that wasn't what she wanted.

Sitting in the bride's room, she stared out the window at the beautiful Texas sky, pondering her decision to wed. Living in Blessing, Texas, there were not many eligible men and if she didn't marry Lester, then who knew if she would ever have the chance to meet and marry another man.

She could be alone. The old maid Walker or the crazy lady in town who children ran from. Living and dying alone.

The sound of voices laughing and joking came to her and she realized it was Lester and his friend Randal Jones, his best man. They sounded drunk.

When she glanced out the window, she saw them staggering toward the church. Lester was handsome, not make-your-knees weak, or even make-your-heart-race good looking. Just a steady man or so she believed.

Her husband to be was inebriated.

But now, the two men were holding each other up, laughing and giggling.

"Are you certain you want to do this," Randal asked. "She's short and chubby."

His words stung. No, she wasn't tall and her figure had often been described as voluptuous. But this monster was calling her fat.

"She's rich," Lester said with a grin. "She's wealthy, and after tonight, I will never have to crawl between her legs again. She thinks we're building a hotel together, but just as soon as I can, I'm headed to the

Black Hills of the Dakota Territory alone. Looking for gold."

He gave an evil laugh and shrugged his shoulders. "Who knows? She could suffer an accident."

Tears sprung in her eyes. Lester was willing to kill her in order to get to her inheritance?

"You dirty dog you," Randal said with a laugh. "Now I understand what you're doing. I don't know if I feel for her or think you're the smartest man I know. Marry the heiress and live off the spoils."

Lester grinned and slapped Randal on the back. "This is why I've been drinking all morning. Look at what I'm marrying. Could you fuck that?"

A gasp escaped her at the coldness of her soon-to-be husband. She hung her head in shame. Was she that ugly? Yes, her hips were wide and she was short, but his words were cruel.

At the thought of his kisses, a shiver ran down her spine. After hearing him talk about her this way, how could she marry him? Sleep with him?

How had she thought that marrying Lester would be right for her?

"Come, on man, let's get in the church, so I can marry this little heifer," he said with a laugh.

A heifer? He thought of her as a cow? And he wanted her to finance their new hotel. The only thing she would finance for Lester was a one-way ticket to hell.

Pain ripped through Bella as she stared around the room where happy brides should be. Tears trickled down her cheeks. What was she doing? Was she willing to settle for a man who obviously didn't love and planned an accident to kill her?

"Oh, hell no," she said suddenly standing. A calmness came over her and a certainty regarding her decision.

She had to get out of here. She had to get away now.

Peeking out the door, she glanced around the church and saw the back entrance. There was no way she was marrying Lester. Not now. Not ever.

When no one was looking, she dashed out the door. Lifting the skirts of her white silk wedding gown, she ran down the street. People out and about cast her an odd glance as she ran to the stable.

Dashing into the barn, she found her horse Midnight.

Quickly she saddled the animal and climbed on. She didn't have a clue where she was going, only that she had to escape the wedding.

She hiked her dress up not caring that someone saw her chubby legs and kicked the horse. To hell with them all.

"Let's go, Midnight. Time to get away. Time to escape."

The horse neighed as they raced out of the stable yard and through the streets of Blessing, Texas. A runaway bride who just needed to ride until she knew where she was going. Until she cleared her head of Lester and his lies.

2

Today was a scorcher. A blazing hot Texas sun beamed down on Jackson Moore as he rode along the road on his trusty gold palomino, his mind wandering back to a place he didn't want to go. The heat was blistering. On long, lazy rides like this one, many a times his mind would betray him and memories overwhelmed him.

Flashes of the smoke and fire and blood. Bodies lying at awkward angles. Flashes of his screams in the night air sweeping him back to that tragic night.

Most of the time, he could keep the torture at bay, but then they would sneak up on him and yank him into the past.

"When we get to Blessing, let's see that woman we were with the last time." Cal Thomas, his partner and friend, brought him back from the dark place his mind slipped into. A place of death and murder.

"Which one?" Jackson said as they rode along, his body

swaying in the saddle. Oak trees and elms lined the road, casting an occasional shadow from the heat of the sun.

"If I remember right Sally."

Jackson didn't say anything, his mind slowly clearing of the scenes of blood everywhere. Coming back to the present where his body occupied.

"Sure," he finally said, knowing any distraction was a good one, but his cock enjoyed their trips to the saloons where they shared a woman. Sometimes a good whore could make a man forget things for a while.

"You know," Cal said, "I've been homesick lately. Susan will never come back, but I miss my ranch. My horses. It's been five years."

Jackson turned and looked at the man he considered his brother. Not by blood, but an even better way. Yes, they were partners, and they shared everything, including women. They both joined the Texas Rangers about the same time, and since then, had become closer than brothers and the only family either of them had in this world.

In fact, Cal had saved Jackson's life. Because surely he would have killed himself after the death of his family. Cal understood when grief and rage consumed him. Only Cal could talk him down from destroying everything in sight. Only he controlled the beast inside Jackson.

But his brother knew grief as well. And in the last two years, Jackson had witnessed Cal finally beginning to come out of his well of despair.

"What are you thinking about doing?"

"I don't know yet. But I want another wife. I want children, grandchildren. I want to wake up every morning with a woman between us. If we found the right woman, we could go home to the ranch and raise horses and cattle. Put this wandering life behind us."

It wasn't a bad idea. In fact, Cal had mentioned it more than once. But Jackson feared getting attached to anyone. They had both suffered losses and just the thought of letting someone close to his heart again terrified him. He couldn't survive losing someone else.

Jackson didn't know what to say. He understood exactly what Cal wanted. At one time, he'd wanted the same thing, but now when the memories of the past took him, he became afraid.

"We've been partners for a long time. I was hoping you'd go with me. There's enough work to keep us both busy," Cal said, glancing at him from under his black cowboy hat. His blonde hair and boyish face always attracted the saloon girls.

But could Jackson give up being a Texas Ranger and living on a ranch? He didn't know.

"I'll think on it. But first you're going to need to find a woman who would understand she belongs to the both of us. That we share everything including her pussy and her ass."

Not many women would accept two men. And giving his heart to a woman would be difficult. How many women would put up with a man who had nightmares, was withdrawn, and frightened of his feelings. Very little chance of a marriage ever happening.

"Oh, Jackson, you're making me hard just thinking

about a beautiful woman spread between us. Me in her cunt and you in her ass."

Jackson pushed the rest of his memories from his mind and concentrated on what Cal was saying. A voluptuous woman, a redhead, a brunette, or his favorite—a blonde, it didn't matter. Someone he could fuck, but never fall in love with, because then his heart would be involved.

"You're just a horny man whose cock is leading him."

Cal laughed. "Yeah, it's been a while. But I want more. I'm tired of saloon girls. I want a good woman to have babies with. A son to leave the ranch to. A daughter who looks like her mother."

Jackson knew that desire. He still owned his family's acreage but he would never return there, not even for a wife and kids. That ground was sanctified. Splattered with the blood of his family.

And though he understood Cal's reasoning for a wife, he couldn't do it. Not now. Maybe not ever. But he didn't want to discourage his brother.

"You find the woman and then we'll talk some more."

Cal was silent for a moment as they rode along, the hot summer sun beating on them.

"Am I wrong to want our wife to be a pure, innocent, virgin?"

How could Jackson ask for a pure woman? He was a broken man. A man whose night terrors often kept him awake until dawn. By no means was he flawless, so he didn't expect his woman to be perfect. She'd be doing good to consider him.

"That's nice, but I'm certainly not perfect and neither are you."

Cal grinned that smile that the ladies all loved. Normally, he found the saloon girl and then Jackson joined in. "No, but a man could wish."

A man could wish for a lot of things, and right now, Jackson just wanted to expunge the demons from his soul, so he would not be a beast.

"Find the right woman and then we'll find out if she's what you wish for. But first we have a killer to capture in Blessing."

They rode along in silence, each lost in his thoughts. Jackson trying to keep the memories at bay. Anything to stop his mind from filling with pictures of their bodies.

But the heat created mirages in his mind, and right now, a black horse with a woman suddenly appeared. He was dreaming.

"Look at that horse," Cal suddenly said. "Something's wrong."

Jackson stared at the black stallion racing wildly toward them. She wasn't a mirage. A woman in a white wedding dress clung to the horse's mane. From all appearances she was either dead or passed out cold.

Cal turned his horse, prepared to intercept the wild looking animal with foam dripping from its mouth. When the stallion came alongside him, he raced to catch him and grabbed the reins, bringing him slowly to a halt.

"Jackson," he yelled. "Get over here."

Gigging his horse, Jackson rode up beside the stallion. A woman wearing a wedding gown was barely hanging on to the bridle, her eyes closed, her blonde hair damp and creamy skin flushed.

One glance at her innocent face and Jackson felt his heart wrench inside his chest. Beautiful, voluptuous, the woman was everything he would have dreamed of in a bride. Everything.

A sense of protectiveness overwhelmed him.

What was she doing out here alone? Suddenly he realized her problem.

"She's overheated. Just like her horse. We've got to cool them down."

"What in the world is a woman in a wedding gown doing on the back of a horse racing like something evil pursued her?"

3

Cal stared at the woman on the back of the black stallion. Had the heavens just answered his prayers? And she'd ridden the stallion without a side saddle. Even now, he could see glimpses of her legs from beneath the silk wedding gown.

"Wow, would you look at this woman? She's beautiful."

"Help me get her and the horse to the river. We've got to cool them both off or they'll die," Jackson said.

Cal knew he was right, but just the sight of her in that wedding dress, her long blonde curls, reddened pale cheeks, and dark lashes that lay against her skin had his cock throbbing. What was wrong?

Was it just the heat?

Cal, still holding the reins, pulled the horse to the river. The stallion who once must have been full of spirit was exhausted. At the river bank, he jumped off his mare and led the stallion into the water.

"Easy, boy. Easy," he said as the animal whinnied in alarm. "We're going to cool you off."

He glanced back and saw Jackson easing the woman off the horse and into the water. "Sorry, darlin', but your wedding gown is going to be ruined."

For a moment, Cal felt a little jealous. While he took care of the horse, his brother was taking care of the woman. Lucky man.

With the blonde in his arms, Jackson waded farther into the river and then gently sat her on a small boulder. About waist deep, Cal watched Jackson as he trickled cool water over her reddened face.

"Oh," she moaned.

"It's all right. You're safe," Jackson promised her. "You and your horse overheated."

Maybe it was better that Jackson was handling the woman. If anyone needed healing, it was him. The man often awoke with nightmares. His screaming would bring Cal out of a dead sleep and then Jackson would pace the room or the woods, wherever they slept for the night.

Cal took his shirt off, soaked it, and then laid it over the animals sweating, twitching back. "Easy boy." He noticed how the horse kept watching Jackson and the woman. "She's all right. Just like you, she needs cooling off."

He dipped the shirt into the water and let it trickle over the horse. His coat was shiny black, his eyes were bright and he could see the feisty spirit in the animal.

The horse tossed its head, its mane shaking droplets of water over Cal. "You think that's funny? I'm supposed to get as wet as you?"

The woman gasped as she came to. Jackson's arms were around her and she struggled to get away.

"Midnight? Where's Midnight?"

She shook her blonde curls and glanced at the two men before she saw her horse. "Thank God, you're safe."

Jackson had her submerged in the water up to her neck. "You and the horse overheated. You could have both died."

"Oh no, my wedding dress," she cried. "It's ruined."

"When is your wedding?" Cal asked.

"It was supposed to be today, but I left the church."

Jackson glanced at Cal. They could have an angry groom looking for her.

"How are you feeling?" Jackson asked, and Cal knew he didn't want to know about a man searching for his bride.

"Better. I did get too hot."

There were so many questions Cal wanted to ask but knew better than appear eager to interrogate her. "Where are you from?"

"Blessing," she said with a sad sigh.

Cal glanced at Jackson stunned. How long had she been riding? She must have left early or ridden very fast.

"That's at least five hours from here," Cal said.

"Unless you ride like a crazy woman. I could have hurt my beautiful horse," she said. "All because I let my emotions get to me."

"We all make mistakes," Jackson said. "But this one could have cost you your life."

"Yes," she replied.

The woman stood in the shallow water, and Cal almost

gasped as the wet white silk clung to the woman's curves. Dear God, she had the most perfect breasts, trim waist, and hips that were full and round enough for a man to grab onto.

With blonde hair and the bluest eyes in the state of Texas, she was gorgeous, and Cal was smitten. Could she be the one for them?

Yet, she had just run out of a wedding.

She walked over to her horse. "Midnight. I'm so glad you're all right. I'm sorry for not taking better care of you."

The horse nuzzled her neck and Cal could see the bond between the animal and its mistress.

Cal noticed that in the last hour, the sun had begun its final descent and the heat was finally beginning to wane. Time to make camp for the night.

"It's too late to return to Blessing tonight. And all of us are soaking wet. We should camp here for the night." It was then he realized she didn't even know who they were and they were telling her they were spending the night together.

"Cal Thomas, Texas Ranger," he said, holding out his hand. "And this is my partner, Jackson Moore."

"Bella Walker," she said biting her lip. "It's just...I should get back to town."

Jackson walked up beside her. "It will be dark. Your horse is tired and what if he steps in a snake hole and snaps a leg. Think of your animal."

She reached out and stroked his coat and Cal wanted her stroking his skin. "It's just that this morning I ran out of the church, leaving my fiancé standing at the altar."

Cal couldn't resist. A grin spread across his face. The woman ran from a wedding right into their arms. Seemed like poetic justice if you asked him.

"Why?" Jackson asked.

In despair, Cal watched as her bottom lip began to tremble and tears streaked down her cheeks. "Because he thought I was ugly."

4

Jackson clenched his fists. The woman's fiancé, her intended, the man marrying her should be protective of the woman he loved. Sure some people married for other reasons, but regardless, it was a man's duty to protect his woman.

And the man must be blind to think she was ugly. The wet silk of her wedding gown showed off her curves to perfection. And it was all he could do not to reach out and touch her breasts. Make her accept that she was stunning.

But could there be more to this story than that? Why would the man consider marrying her if he didn't like the way she looked? Something was off. Way off.

"Why don't we set up camp and then you can tell us all about your fiancé," Jackson said.

He glanced at Cal and knew the man felt the same way.

Jackson helped her from the river and she glanced down at the dress she'd been wearing. "What a shame that I ruined a beautiful wedding gown."

Night was fast approaching and the frogs were beginning to sing as the cicadas cried out. It was Jackson's favorite time of the day. When everyone was preparing for nighttime. And even the animals were calling for a mate.

"Better the dress than being attached to a man who doesn't want or love you," Cal said leading Midnight from the water.

She patted the horse's coat. "I know but look at me and the dress. I'm not pretty and now I look even worse."

Jackson stopped and turned toward her. He stared into her sapphire eyes and saw the pain radiating. At first, he wasn't certain the woman really meant the words she said, but after seeing the tears welling up in her eyes, he knew she believed the nonsense.

He took her hands and gazed into her eyes, and it was at that moment, Jackson knew she was the woman for them. A sense of possessiveness overwhelmed him, and though he feared giving anyone his heart, he wanted Bella. Needed her.

And she needed them.

With a shake of his head, he couldn't believe his own thoughts. Today when Cal mentioned finding a wife, he never dreamed she would appear over the next hill.

"Honey, the dress may be ruined, but you are beautiful. I'm not just saying this to make you feel better. You are a woman who a man would be crazy not to love and adore. Your blue eyes remind me of the sky and your lips are perfect for kissing. And your body was created by God to tempt man."

Her bottom lip trembled and it was all he could do not to grab her and kiss her.

"But he said he could never fuck me," she gasped.

Cal let out an exasperated sound. "The man's an idiot. Too stupid to see the beauty right in front of him. Darling, you are perfect."

She sniffed and glanced between the two men. "You're just being nice. No man in town would court me. I was all alone until Lester began to flirt with me."

The two men surrounded her, putting her between them. "Don't believe anything the man said to you."

In the circle of their bodies, he hoped she felt protected, cared for.

"Let's get camp set up for the night. Feed that horse of yours and ours and then we'll talk more. You can tell us what happened."

She hugged first Jackson, sending his heart to pounding in his chest and his dick rose and pressed hard against his wet pants. There could've been steam rising from the front of them. Then she turned and gave Cal a hug.

The two men exchanged a knowing look. They were both eager to take her and make her theirs.

"You both have been so good to me. First saving my life and my horse's life and now making me feel better."

If only she knew what Jackson really wanted to do. Lay her on the ground, spread her legs, and sample her sweet pussy. But she had been hurt. He pushed aside his wayward thoughts and focused on setting up camp.

"We'll gather firewood and set up our tent for the night," Cal said, reading his mind.

"What can I do to help?" she asked.

"You can sit down and rest. You tested your body today and you should take it easy," Jackson said, knowing he needed a break from seeing her in that clinging silk gown that now had water stains on it. It wasn't the dress, but the curves that the satin clung to like a second skin that had his dick screaming for attention.

"Thank you," she said. "I am rather tired."

Jackson and Cal had worked together long enough that they fell into their routine. Soon, Cal had a frying pan out and busy heating up hard tack and jerky. Jackson had set up their small tent, taking the two sleeping rolls for them to all sleep on together.

Already, his mind had gone to her curvaceous body squeezed between the two of them. He couldn't wait for tonight.

5

As the last rays of the sun begin to sink below the western sky, Bella's dress was soaking wet. Her undergarments were wet and though it was in the heat of summer, she felt herself start to shake.

"You're cold," Jackson replied, staring at her as he made them supper. "I think you should take the dress off and your undergarments and hang them up to dry."

A shiver went through Bella, but it wasn't from the cold, but rather these two handsome cowboys. She couldn't decide which one she liked better, Jackson or Cal. They were both rugged-looking men that when she gazed at them a trickle of heat spiraled through her and ended right between her legs.

And tonight she would be staying with them. Sharing their tent.

As much as she tried, she didn't know which she preferred. Each man had a unique personality. Jackson was the quieter one, but when he glanced at her, the urge to remove her clothes almost overwhelmed her. There was something about his dark sensuous gaze that made her want to melt naked in his arms.

And Cal. The man was friendly with a kind personality that made you want to cuddle up next to him.

Both of them made her feel things she'd never experienced. Never. Especially not with Lester.

She bit her lip knowing she never responded to Jackson as a second shiver went through her. Maybe it was shock. Maybe it was fear, but whatever it was, her bones were almost rattling.

"I have an extra shirt you can wear."

"What will you wear?"

"I'm fine," he said as he stood and walked to his saddle bags and pulled out a long sleeve shirt. "Put it on and let your clothes hang to dry."

"But I'll have no underpants?"

"Darling, that shirt is going to hang down to your knees."

It was scandalous, but maybe she needed to live a little more dangerously than she had in the past. Maybe being a prim and proper woman had led her to agree to marry a man she didn't love. Someone who wanted to kill her if they were married.

Those words still shocked her.

She took the shirt from Cal and walked into the bushes. As she pulled the wet silk down her skin, disappointment filled her. The dress had been beautiful, the party afterward would have been perfect and yet the day turned out nothing like she'd planned.

And now, here she was out on the Texas prairie with two strangers, almost naked and both of them made her think of things she'd never thought before.

With trepidation, she pulled her wet chemise and pantaloons from her body. They were soaked and quickly she placed his dry shirt over her naked body. They were Texas Rangers, men she could trust. Men who would not take advantage of her.

Even though she was beginning to think she wanted them too. The thought of their hands on her, touching, caressing her skin sent heat spiraling through her. What was wrong with her to think of them in that way? Maybe because tonight she thought she would be losing her virginity. She thought she would become a woman. She thought her groom desired her, not thought of her as a heifer.

Pain gripped her chest as she remembered his words. Why did they hurt so much?

She was tired of waiting for a man to come along. A decent man. Someone who would love her.

Timidly she stepped out of the bushes and walked closer to the fire and hung her gown and undergarments in the bushes. This could be dangerous, but she'd already faced down danger once today.

Cal let out of soft whistle. "Honey, you look like a fine peach, ripe for the picking."

Jackson went into the bushes and when he returned, his shirt was off and he had put on dry pants. He laid his garments in the bushes next to hers.

Her mouth suddenly went dry as she watched his

muscles ripple as he moved and she had the strangest urge to run her hand down the front of his chest. To touch all that naked flesh. Those hardened muscles.

Cal disappeared into the bushes and when he returned, she stared. He was wearing no pants, just long johns that outlined his firm thighs, his penis snug against his body.

"Sorry, but everything was wet," he said.

Jackson shook his head, and a tingle of awareness went through Bella. He walked toward her and then she felt Jackson at her back.

"You have nothing to fear from us," Cal said.

She believed him. It was like she could sense his goodness and knew that no matter what happened, both of these men would protect her.

They sandwiched her between them and she glanced up into Cal's dark brown eyes. He reached out and let his hand trail down her arm to her hand. "You're beautiful, Bella. Never forget that you're every man's dream."

"You're just saying that to be nice," she said.

"No, we don't say things we don't mean," Jackson said, his voice low from behind her sent a trickle of heat through her. Reaching around her, he cupped her breast causing her to gasp as fire exploded inside her. "Your breasts are the perfect size."

Cal's hands gripped her waist and he grinned as he slid them down to her hips. "Your waist is small making your hips curve in the right places."

Jackson's hand slid between her legs and he cupped

her pussy and her mouth dropped open. Had she been wrong about them?

"Your sweet pussy is dripping with need. You're a beautiful woman," Jackson said as his mouth moved along her neck kissing the curve, while his fingers did the most delicious thing she'd ever felt. Sliding along her inner folds creating a firestorm as a moan escaped her and her knees began to buckle.

"What are you doing?"

"Showing you that you're gorgeous and that any man would be lucky to have you," Jackson whispered in her ear.

Cal moved closer and his mouth claimed hers, his lips consuming, causing heat to burst in her core as Jackson's fingers pushed inside her. Standing between them, her knees buckled as a fire blazed through her body.

What was happening to her? Why did she feel so good with fire racing through her veins?

"Oh Cal, she's a virgin. I can feel her maiden head in her sweet pussy."

Cal's lips slowly ceased to kiss her. "Finish her off and then let's talk."

Finish her off? What did he mean by that?

Jackson's fingers moved faster over her clit, stroking, creating an intensity inside her that she didn't understand. Hot need built inside her. A pressure of something she craved but couldn't grasp raced through her.

"Come for me, darling," he whispered in her ear as his deep voice sent even more heat down her spine.

A whimper escaped her as she laid her back against Jackson's naked chest.

Cal leaned forward, brushed the shirt aside and laid his mouth against her nipple. With a gentle nip, Bella's body suddenly tensed, her body going into a spasm as she cried out.

"Jackson, what's happening?"

He held her body tightly against his own and she felt his manhood press into her buttocks as her body shook, and she cried out in pleasure.

With a sigh, she collapsed in a faint.

6

Bella was their woman. No doubt resided in Cal's mind as he watched Jackson lay her in the tent. Cal's dick felt ready to explode with need as he'd watched her orgasm right before his eyes.

She was a virgin and she was so damn beautiful, he'd wanted to fuck her the moment he saw her. It was like fate put her right in front of them, saying *here is your woman.*

If Jackson agreed, he would ask her to marry him tonight. And if she said yes, he would taste her sweet cunny before the night ended. Then first thing in the morning, they would be married.

He had been alone for so many years and sweet Bella would hopefully soon be his and Jackson's. His brother came out of the tent.

"Poor thing, today took its toll on her. She's fast asleep."

"I want to marry her," Cal said, his dick throbbing, just thinking of her lying in their tent, nearly naked. The woman was beautiful, he was attracted to her and it was all he could do not to crawl into the tent and show her just how much he longed for her. But he was a good man and he would wait.

Jackson smiled. "We just met her."

The fire popped, sending sparks flying into the air. The smell of a wood fire was always something Cal enjoyed. It was why he did most of the cooking.

"She's in trouble. She needs us. Right now, I want to ride into Blessing and kill that mother fucker who did this to her."

"And then you'd go to prison," Jackson said. "Believe me, it wouldn't take much for me to put a bullet in him."

"If he called her ugly, could he have another reason to marry her?"

"Don't know," Jackson said. "But she's seems nervous whenever you try to talk about him. And she hasn't told us his name."

"True." Cal sat in front of the fire. "You don't think it's a good idea to make her ours?"

"My fingers were in her sweet cunt. What do you think?"

A grin spread across Cal's face. "I was so envious."

It was true, he wanted to shove his friend out of the way and take his turn, but that wouldn't have been polite and it would possibly scare Bella. And he had a proposition for her.

A frown spread across Jackson's face. "You know my past. I'm afraid to give my heart to anyone. You marry her and then I'll be free to leave if I need to."

This was not surprising, but Cal thought Jackson

should be the legal husband if she accepted their proposal. Marriage might heal Jackson or possibly destroy him. But still, Jackson was his best friend, his brother, and Cal hoped someday he'd be able to put this behind him.

And yet, he also realized that by taking a wife, he was leaving himself open to hurt. He'd lost one wife; could he risk losing a second? But this was what he wanted more than anything.

Bella was his future.

"We'll explain our life to her and see if she's willing to take a chance on us. If not, then we'll help her as much as she will allow. But if she agrees, I'm tasting her sweet pussy tonight."

Jackson smiled. "But we will not fuck her until one of us is married to her."

"Agreed," Cal said. "I'm praying she'll agree."

Jackson sat on the log beside Cal. "Damn, we could be married this time tomorrow."

"Yes," Jackson said.

"How long should we let her sleep?"

"Until she wakes up," Jackson said. "Or until I can't stand it any longer."

Cal laughed. "Maybe the smell of food will awaken her."

"Maybe," Jackson said.

An hour later, Cal was pacing around the fire when he finally heard Bella stirring. When she walked out of the tent, he thought he'd never seen a more beautiful sight and he hoped that soon, he would wake up every morning to her by his side.

Her hair was tossed, her eyes were sleepy, her lips ripe for kissing and yet she was gorgeous. Why she believed the louse and his wrong opinions, he didn't know. Sure her hips were well rounded, but that was exactly what he liked in a woman. Something to hang onto.

"Are you hungry?" Jackson asked.

"Yes," she said softly, pulling the shirt around her tightly. Soon he hoped that shirt would be tossed inside the tent and he could gaze at every inch of her naked body from her full lush breasts to her pussy.

Cal handed her a piece of warmed hard tack and she sat on the log.

"Thank you," she said and gazed up at the stars. "How long did I sleep?"

"Maybe an hour. You're still recovering," Jackson said.

How did Cal go about asking her to marry him? It had been easy the first time, but this time, he didn't know her as well as Susan and yet he wanted her so badly.

Cal stepped in front of her and then kneeled down beside her. "Bella, you've had a rough day. And maybe this isn't the best time to ask you, but we feel like it's important. You could be in danger."

"I know," she said and tears welled up in her eyes. "He's a bastard."

There had to be something she wasn't telling them, for her to agree that she was in danger. Had he threatened her somehow?

"We want to protect you. We want to make certain that this asshole can never try to hurt you again. We want to be your men."

"My men?"

"Yes, you see Jackson and I share everything. We've been talking about finding us a wife. You need a husband. But you have to understand that you would be marrying not just one of us, but both of us. We would share you."

Her mouth opened into a perfect shaped O and Cal imagined those full lips of hers wrapped around his cock. It would be so hard to refrain from fucking her tonight.

"We know it's an unusual arrangement, but this way if something happened to one of us, you would have the other man to still protect you and our family."

"You want children?"

"Most definitely," Cal said. "The sooner the better. I want a large family."

"Me too," she said and then turned to Jackson. "Is this what you want?"

"Darling, I want to fuck you so bad, but I'm a free spirit. If you agree, Cal will marry you. We'll share you and I'll always be there for you, but I can never give you my heart."

She tilted her head and glanced at each man. "I appreciate your honesty. What about you Cal? Will you give me your heart?"

"Honey, yes. It may take some time, but I want you to love me, heart and soul, and I'll do the same. Understand that when we say we'll share you, one of us will take you in your pussy and one will take you in your ass. You will always be our woman, and if you don't obey us, we will punish you."

"How?"

"I will put you over my knee and paddle your ass," Cal said.

"And I will as well," Jackson replied.

Cal took her hand. "Will you marry us, Bella, and be our woman?"

A grin spread across her face. "Yes. When are we getting married?"

Both men smiled. "In the morning. But tonight, we're going to celebrate."

7

Bella didn't know what to believe. They told her she was beautiful, and yet, she didn't feel that way. And they had seen her at her worst. Her hair down, wet, sweating, and they told her she was perfect for them.

Who did she believe? These men or Lester?

And was she crazy for agreeing to marry them? They had just met. Yet, there was a certainty about them. Like this was where she belonged.

All she wanted in life was a family. A man who loved her and their children. Someone who would look after her and their family. She had not been able to find that in Blessing. No men would court her.

These two strangers wanted to make her their wife, yet they wanted to share her. They were Texas Rangers, so they must be good men, but what did she know about them?

As they finished their meal, she turned to Jackson, who with one look from his dark emerald eyes and black lashes, sent heat spiraling through her body and her lungs seized in her chest. Never had a man affected her this way. Never had she felt the urge to curl around a hard muscled chest, spread her legs, and give herself to a man.

Her tongue swiped across her dry lips as she gazed at him. If they were to marry, she needed to know about them. About their backgrounds, their families. Anything they would tell her.

"Tell me about yourself. Do you have family?" she asked them.

A flash of hurt crossed Jackson's face and his chiseled jaw tightened. The urge to reach out and caress his cheek was strong as she gazed into those eyes losing herself in his stare.

"I'm alone."

Something about the way he said it alerted her. There was pain in his expression. A hurt that she felt reached down to his soul. Tonight, he wouldn't tell her, but maybe someday when he trusted her.

"Me too," she says softly. "I'm all alone. My parents are dead. No brothers or sisters. Not even aunts or uncles nearby."

Jackson reached out and pulled her into his arms. "Not anymore."

She glanced up at him and the urge to kiss him overwhelmed her. As if he understood her need, he leaned down, his lips covering hers. The kiss was urgent, like their hearts had called out to one another as she gave herself to the feelings the kiss evoked.

This was what she wanted. What she needed.

When they broke apart, she gazed into his eyes and knew he would not tell her what happened to his family. Knowing she needed to know more about each of them, she tried to move off his lap, but he held her tightly.

"Stay," he said softly as he nuzzled her ear.

Heat flooded through her as she sat on his lap, her bottom against to the hard ridge in his pants.

"What about you, Cal? Any family?"

"They're all scattered about doing their own thing back east. There is one thing you need to know. I was married once before."

"What happened?"

"A rattlesnake bit her one evening while she was in the garden. The poison took her by morning," he said with a sigh. "She's buried on the property."

Bella felt her heart tug with sadness. Cal had loved and lost someone. Her parents died so quickly from a respiratory ailment. First her mother, and then her father, leaving her alone, devastated. Her chest tightened at the memory, and how in the following months, she learned to live on her own.

Alone.

She reached out her hand and he moved over to join her and Jackson. "I'm sorry."

"After Susan died, I packed up and left the ranch in the capable hands of my foreman. Joined up with the Texas Rangers and there I met Jackson."

Bella glanced between the two men. "How do you know that the two of you can share me? What if one of you tires of sharing and decides you want your own woman?"

Jackson put his hand on her chin and turned her face to him. "In a sense, we're brothers. We've fought alongside one another, protected each other, and saved each other's lives a time or two. We have no secrets from each other. And when you marry us, we will protect and cherish you. You will want for nothing."

It all sounded so wonderful and yet she felt uncertain about sharing two men. How would it work?

"What's troubling you," Cal asked. "Have you changed your mind?"

"No," she said. "I've never heard of two men sharing one woman. And yet, I find you both attractive and could never choose between you."

A smile crossed Cal's face. "That's what I like to hear. Maybe if we show you, you'll understand better."

Her heart sped inside her chest, racing at the thought of what they would show her.

"We're not married," she said breathless with anticipation.

"And we'll wait to take your maidenhead until we've said our vows," Jackson said. "You'll be Cal's legal wife, but those vows will be written on my heart just as if I'd said them."

Cal stood and took her hand, pulling her to her feet. "Until then, there are other ways for us to join. To give you pleasure. Your body is ours and we're going to make you scream when you come. If we don't, then we haven't done our job."

She gazed into his brown eyes and shivered at the

desire she saw there. Jackson stood and moved behind her, pressing his hard cock into her backside.

"You'll both take me at the same time?" she asked her voice quiet, not certain of how that would work.

"Eventually," Cal said. "We'll train you in our likes and give you boundless pleasure."

Jackson slid his hands around to her front and grasped her breasts. "And when your belly is swollen with our child, we'll be thrilled. No more being alone. A family of our own."

"Yes," she gasped as Cal stepped in close to her and grabbed her pussy.

"This pussy is ours. Your ass is ours and you're our woman. Disobey and you will be punished."

Bella's mouth went dry. How could she disobey them? Weren't they all adults?

Cal suddenly lifted her and threw her over his shoulder. "Time to show you, we're your men."

Her heart pounded and she thought back to how they had pleasured her this afternoon. Would they do the same or something different. They said they would not take her maidenhead until they were married, and yet, she knew they had something planned.

Bouncing on his shoulder, she felt relief when they reached the small tent and he laid her inside on their sleeping rolls.

"Take the shirt off," Jackson said. "We want to see your body."

Sitting up, she slowly unbuttoned the shirt all the way

and then she let it slip from her shoulders, exposing her naked breast and pussy.

In the deepening twilight, she gazed at them and then lay back on the pallet. "Take your clothes off."

She was just as excited to see their hardened muscles and rigid cocks as they were to see her body. In fact, she had never seen a man's penis before except in a forbidden school textbook.

Now she would get to see the real thing. When they finished shedding their clothes, she gazed in awe at the way both of their cocks were long and hard. Though similar in size and shape, each man's manhood had a different curve and width.

And eventually they would each take her.

Kneeling on the blankets, they each took a leg and spread her open.

Cal kneeled between her knees, and with shock, she watched as his mouth descended upon her pussy. Jackson leaned down and took her breast in his mouth. Both sensations hit her at once and she gasped.

"Cal, what are you doing?"

"Pleasuring your cunty," Jackson said between sucking on her nipples.

Cal raised his head. "Tonight is about you."

She felt his mouth suck her clit between his lips and then his teeth gently nipped her, sending sensations rushing through her as her fists gripped the sleeping roll.

"Oh, Cal," she cried. "Please."

Jackson's teeth nipped her nipple and she almost came

up off the blankets. She grabbed his head and held it to her breasts not letting him get away as ripples of pure pleasure cascaded through her. A mounting tension filled her and she raised her hips needing something she didn't understand.

Cal's hand slapped her pussy and the sting sent her spiraling over the edge.

"Cal," she screamed as her body tightened and she gripped the fingers he had shoved inside her. Pleasure rippled through her.

They didn't give her a break as she floated down to earth, but rather switched positions.

"She has the sweetest tasting pussy, and I think she liked it when I spanked her there."

Jackson dove between her legs, but he was different from Cal. He spread her legs farther and raised them up on his shoulders, opening her up wider as his tongue slid over her folds, caressing each one. Spending a lot of time on the little nerve filled bud.

A moan escaped from Bella as once again she could feel the pressure begin to build. Cal's mouth covered hers, his tongue invading her mouth, dancing with hers as Jackson tongued her folds.

His fingers opened her and he shoved his tongue inside her as far as it would go, lapping around inside her pussy, holding her so that she couldn't move, sending heat flooding through her.

A gasp escaped her.

Once again, she could feel the pleasure mounting within her and she couldn't escape. Between the way that

Cal was kissing her and the way Jackson was tonguing her, her body began to tremble.

"Don't come, baby," Cal said, releasing her lips. "Hold it."

A moan escaped her and she clenched the blankets, knowing she couldn't hold back much longer.

Then she felt his finger trailing over her ass and she froze. They said they would train her, but she didn't expect them to do this now.

"Relax," Jackson said. "Let me in."

He spread her juices around her ass and then he slid one finger into her ass.

"Aargh," she cried. Not because it hurt, but it seemed so shameful.

"It's all right," Cal said against her ear as he lifted her arms and put them above her head, holding them there. "Jackson is going to make you feel so good."

Slowly he began to push his fingers in and out while his tongue continued the assault on her clit and pussy. The sensations grew until she knew she could not hold back any longer.

"Please," she cried.

Jackson added a second digit and that's when she screamed her pleasure, unable to hold off any longer.

"Jackson," she cried. "Oh, Jackson."

His whole mouth consumed her clit and she whimpered. "Please fuck me."

"Sorry, baby," Cal said as she lay trembling on the ground. Jackson moved up next to her and they placed her between them.

"This is where you belong," Jackson said facing her. "Between your men."

Bella's breathing was rough as she reached out to Jackson. "Oh, I want you inside me so bad."

"Not tonight," Jackson said. "But you did come without permission."

She glanced up at him, staring into his emerald eyes that were dark with desire. "I couldn't hold back any longer."

"When we tell you to wait, we mean it," Cal said.

Cal sat up and then together they pulled her over his lap.

"We'll go easy on you this time. Only five licks," Jackson said. "And one on the pussy."

They couldn't be serious. She glanced back and forth between the two men. "You're going to spank me for having an orgasm?"

"Yes, we are," Cal said. "Now lay across my lap."

Reluctantly, she slowly moved until she was lying across Cal's lap, his cock against her belly. If only she could slip down a little farther maybe she could distract him.

"Count with me," he said.

Thinking about how it would feel to have his cock in her pussy, she was unprepared for the first lick.

Crack!

"Ouch," she cried.

"Count, baby," Jackson said as his fingers begin to work their magic once again on her folds.

This wasn't fair. They were teasing her while they spanked her.

"One," she gasped as he twisted her clit. How could a spanking create so much desire? She felt like she was on fire again. Not only in her buttocks, but between her legs.

Crack!

"Two," she said, suddenly realizing that the warmth spreading from her cheeks to her pussy.

Crack!

"Oh, three," she said as she moved back, wanting to give Jackson's fingers more access. Needing that soothing touch that heated her, knowing if they kept this up, she would be coming again.

Crack!

"Four," she gasped, her breathing harsh. Her body tensed, the pleasure building once again. What if she came without their permission again? Would they spank her again?

Crack!

"Five," she cried. "I'm going to come."

"Hold it, or we will do this again," Cal said.

Bella gritted her teeth, knowing that there was one more slap, waiting, anticipating. Jackson rolled her to her back.

He slapped her pussy full on. "Come, Bella, come."

Her screams filled the tent as the orgasm carried her over the edge unlike anything she had experienced.

"I think our wife likes to be spanked," Cal said with a grin as he stared down at Bella who lay drained. This was nothing like what she had imagined her life would be like. This was so much better.

"I think you're right," Jackson said as he pulled her up against him and cradled her.

Drained, Bella lay against his naked chest. Maybe being a runaway bride had its advantages.

Maybe she had found two men to love and cherish her.

8

The next morning it had taken them nearly five hours to ride into Blessing. After a leisurely morning with their naked soon-to-be bride, they finally packed up and rode into town.

Bella insisted they go to her home and clean up. Their bride had a nice house in the middle of the town, close to everything.

They still had an investigation to conduct and this would be a great headquarters for them to return to each night. He had no idea how they were going to locate this killer, but so far he had killed three women. The sheriff specifically requested that the Texas Rangers be brought in.

Now they were here, but not how they planned on getting to Blessing. Today was their wedding day. Today was the day they claimed Bella as theirs. And Jackson could hardly wait.

Though he would not be her legal husband, he would

claim her. But somehow he had to protect his heart, because he could not take another death. So he would be her detached husband. The one who would not tell her he loved her.

After they arrived, Bella ordered her housekeeper to heat a bath and had retreated to her bedroom to prepare for the ceremony.

Cal was dressed and waiting while Jackson prepared.

He crawled into Bella's tub after she left and had taken advantage of cleaning up. It felt good to no longer be sweaty and dirty. He even fit into one of her father's suits. Cal didn't want to wear a suit, but rather just a good pair of clean pants and a decent shirt.

Jackson felt confused about how much to tell Bella about his past. Last night, Bella had come apart in their arms. She'd been vulnerable, teachable, and trusting most of all.

While he couldn't tell her what happened to his family, they shared the commonality of death. And that left him vulnerable to her. Because he couldn't talk about his loss. He couldn't tell her that he came home and found them all dead. Yet, he felt a connection with her that he feared.

Because he could never let another person into his heart that was so badly damaged.

"Are you ready?"

She came around the corner dressed in a blue gown that clung to her curves, her blonde curls loose as they flowed down her back. The urge to wrap her hair in his fists and bring her lips to his almost overcame him. But once he started, he wouldn't be able to stop.

How could anyone call their woman ugly? How could she believe she was not beautiful?

He stepped toward her, took her hands, and leaned back. "Frankly, I like this dress better than the one you planned to marry in. You're stunning, gorgeous, and I'm a lucky man to have you for a wife."

A smile spread across her face and her blue eyes filled with tears. "You don't have to lie to me."

Anger welled up quickly inside him. "I will never lie to you. You're beautiful and don't you ever forget it."

Cal walked over. He raised her dress and slapped her on the ass.

"Cal," she cried, her face turning a brilliant shade of pink.

"If it wasn't our wedding day, you would get more. We will never lie to you about anything. And I don't want to ever hear you say you're not beautiful. Do you understand?"

A frown crossed her face. "Yes."

"Now let's go to the church. We have a wedding night to get to."

Cal took her by the arm and they walked out the door. Jackson followed behind as they made their way down Main Street to the church at the edge of town.

The people they passed stopped and turned their heads, staring.

"There she is," one man said.

A woman harrumphed. "Just like that, she's back. Poor Lester."

Lester? Was he her intended?

Jackson chose to ignore the comments knowing if he said anything it would only draw more attention. And until Bella was theirs, he didn't want any trouble.

The white building with a bell tower stood at the far end of town. The building must have been there for years as the paint was faded, not the brilliant white it once was.

Stepping up the wooden stairs, they entered the church. Stained glass windows ran along the wall of the chapel. A large wooden cross hung in the front. It was a beautiful church and yet the last time Jackson had been inside a house of worship was when he buried his family.

Bella gave a visible shiver.

"Are you all right?" Jackson asked, wondering if her nerves were getting the better of her.

Yesterday she'd been going to marry Lester and today she was marrying Cal.

"Yes, bad memories flooded me of overhearing Lester and running out the door." She tossed her blonde hair over her shoulders

"No one is going to hurt you," Cal assured her and Jackson knew they were in agreement. "You're not nervous?"

"No," she said with strength and warmth. Their woman was ready to become their wife.

They'd fight to the death to protect their woman, their soon-to-be wife.

"Can I help you—Bella, you're safe. What happened? You disappeared on your wedding day."

A man in a suit with a white collar approached them.

"I'm sorry, Pastor, but I couldn't marry Lester," she said.

"Why not?"

Cal put his hand on her back. "Because she's going to marry me."

Jackson was glad that Cal didn't let her tell the pastor why the wedding didn't happen. Something warned him about this Lester. His gut told him this guy was not a good man. And he must be blind if he didn't think Bella was beautiful.

"Will you marry us?" Bella asked.

The man looked stunned. "How long have you known each other?"

"I'm a Texas Ranger. We met on the road and just found each other," Cal told the preacher man.

The man seemed stunned.

"Are you sure about this, Bella?"

"Yes, I am. If you won't marry us in a church, then we'll go to the courthouse. But we're getting married today," she said with a determination that Jackson loved.

Whatever doubts she had last night, they were gone and she wanted to be their wife.

Happiness spread through Jackson, and before it could reach his heart, he shut it down. He would fuck her and care for her, but nothing further. He couldn't. The thought of losing her was more than he could survive. So, logically, if he didn't give her his love, then if something happened, he would live.

"All right, let me grab my Bible and we'll have a wedding."

A smile spread across her face, and while the preacher was gone, she took first Cal's hand and then Jackson's.

"Thank you," she said. "I'm so excited to begin our life together."

"Me too," Cal said.

As much as he wanted to deny his feelings he couldn't. "Me as well."

He was excited about Bella being their wife. No matter what happened, he just had to protect his heart from being involved. Hopefully, Cal would help her to understand.

The preacher reappeared. "Are we ready?"

"Yes," Bella said as she walked beside Cal to the front of the church.

Thirty minutes later, they walked outside to a gathering crowd. The sheriff stood in the front waiting.

9

Bella was theirs. Cal was the happiest man alive as they walked out of the church onto the streets of Blessing. Until he saw the waiting crowd.

The sheriff stood in front of the people as they stood staring, watching them, not at all friendly. About twenty people were gathered behind the sheriff, glaring at them like they had stolen her and they were prepared to string Cal up in the nearest tree.

"Bella," the lawman called, "where have you been? I've had a posse out searching for you."

The people murmured quietly as the evening sun set in the western sky, casting an orange glow about the town. From the expressions on the people's faces, they were angry.

"I'm sorry, Sheriff. I couldn't marry Lester and I took off," Bella said.

Cal was glad she didn't tell the town what happened

between her and her ex-fiancé. No need to get gossip started and rile the man.

A frown crossed his face. "Who are these gentlemen?"

Cal stepped forward. "Cal Thomas, Texas Ranger, Bella's new husband."

A gasp came from the crowd and people begin to whisper.

"Jackson Moore, Texas Ranger," Jackson said as he stepped forward and shook the man's hand.

A smile crossed his face. "Seth Ingram, former Texas Ranger, sheriff of Blessing."

Relief filled Cal. Now he felt certain they wouldn't have to fight the man and the town regarding Bella. A horse and carriage rolled down the street past the crowd kicking up dust, but no one moved.

"You sent for us," Jackson said.

"Yes," Seth replied. "Why don't you gentleman come to my office tomorrow morning and we'll discuss the cases I want to talk with you about."

A man after Cal's own heart. He knew tonight was their wedding night and he was giving them an out. A chance to explore their bride's body and sink their cocks into her sweet willing pussy.

A man charged through the crowd, pushing people out of the way. "Where is she? Where is that bitch?"

Cal shoved Bella behind him, and Jackson moved in close to protect her. He would have to go through both of them to reach her. And nothing would give Cal more pleasure than to let his fist connect with the man's face.

A tall, dark haired man wearing a stained white apron

burst in front of them, his icy blue eyes flashed with rage, his face held a grimace that even Cal stepped back from.

This was the man she was engaged to.

"You left me at the altar, Bella."

Bella calmly stared at him. "You're right I did. I overheard you talking to your friend, Randal. You didn't want to marry me. You wanted my money."

The crowd begin to back away from Lester. Before they had been on his side, but now Cal could see them giving the man a wide berth.

"You said some terrible things about me," Bella said quietly staring the man down. Her fists clenched and he could tell she was controlling the anger she felt for her former fiancé.

"You humiliated me," he said. "I'm going to—"

He raised his fists and approached her and the sound of a gun being cocked halted him.

Jackson's body was tense, his gun hand steady as he pointed the weapon at Lester.

"She's married to Cal. Don't even think about hitting her or you're a dead man. No one for any reason should hit a woman, especially with his fists clenched. You've overstepped your bounds."

People in the crowd shook their heads, their anger growing.

The man retreated and slowly lowered his fists. His face contorted with rage. And Cal knew they now had an enemy in town.

"You're mistaken. I loved you, Bella. I was drunk when I said those things. I don't want your money."

Cal wasn't buying his excuses. Liquor had a way of making a man talk. Of saying things that were true, that he really should've kept to himself.

"There was more to that conversation, but I'm not going to say the words in front of this crowd. We're over. Now I'm married to Cal."

Lester glared at Cal and then at Jackson. "You stole my bride. How do you know they didn't marry you for your money? I didn't want your riches. Hell, I was willing to overlook your plump, ugly body—"

The crowd gasped and Cal glanced at Bella whose face wilted.

"Don't say another word," Cal said his voice, deep and low, "or I will punch you into next week. This conversation is over. Stay away from my wife unless you want the law looking for you."

The urge to pummel the man until he couldn't walk was strong in Cal, but he tried to contain his composure. Right now, they had the town on their side. If Lester came near Bella, all bets were off. The man wouldn't be walking away.

Bella was not plump or ugly. The man was only belittling her because he knew it hurt her fragile feelings. In thirty seconds, he'd undone everything Cal and Jackson said to make her feel beautiful. And she was curvaceous and gorgeous and everything they wanted in a woman.

"Get the hell out of my sight before I decide to kick your ass," Jackson said.

That's why they made such a good team. They backed up each other.

The sheriff stood glancing at the man shaking his head, a smile on his face. When Lester turned to leave, an older woman spat at his feet.

"Never talk about a woman that way. I don't care what she's done to you," she growled at him. "You're not a good man. Now get out of my sight."

The man curled his lip as he walked away from the crowd. For now, it was over, but somehow Cal felt certain they had not seen the last of him.

Several of the woman walked over to Bella.

"Dear, you dodged a bullet when you left that church. Congratulations on your wedding." The older woman looked Cal up and down. "Your new husband is a looker. Treat her right or you're going to answer to the women in this town."

A grin spread across Cal's face as he nodded to the woman. "Don't worry, she'll be treated well. My beautiful wife deserves to be happy."

The woman smiled at him and the other women around her sighed.

"A true love story," said one woman. "He rescued her from Lester. Who knew Lester was so mean and vile?"

Jackson stood off to the side of the street, watching Lester who had disappeared into the local cafe. "He's gone."

"Good. Now, if you'll excuse us, tonight is our wedding night. And I have a special dinner planned for my bride."

The women grinned their approval.

The older woman took Bella's hands in hers. "We're so happy for you, dear. Your parents would approve."

Cal took her arm and led her away from the women. Jackson followed and it was all Cal could do to keep from running down the street to her home.

Tonight they would make her theirs. Tonight they would claim her.

What Bella didn't know was the housekeeper had fixed them dinner, leaving behind the special dessert he asked for. A dessert that he would share with his bride and Jackson while they fucked.

10

As soon as they walked into the house, her husbands turned to gaze at her. Cal kissed her. "Go into the bedroom and remove your clothes."

"But we haven't eaten dinner yet," she said, anticipating the night, wanting it to be special. Watching her men stand up for her left her feeling good. They protected her from Lester and his ugliness.

"And we will with you naked," Jackson said.

Her mouth dropped open and she smiled. Why she felt nervous, she didn't know, but she never dreamed of them wanting her to eat without her clothes on.

"All right," she said and walked upstairs to the bedroom. Quickly she removed her clothes and when she returned to the dining room, there were candles lit and their dinner was all set out.

"Who did this?" she asked, knowing that the men didn't cook.

"Your housekeeper cooked for us," Cal said.

Jackson sat at the table. "Come here and sit on my lap."

Why he wanted her to sit on his lap at the table, she didn't know, but she did as he asked. They were married and she felt guilty that Jackson could not say that she belonged to him.

Both men made her body tingle in places she'd never experienced.

Once she was seated on his lap the way he wanted her, which was with her side to the table, Cal took a piece of cloth and wrapped it around her eyes, blindfolding her.

"What are you doing?" she asked, a tingle of excitement zipping along her spine.

"Just relax and enjoy tonight," Cal said, leaning down next to her ear. "We're going to make you feel so good."

Suddenly a fork was at her lips and Jackson, or maybe it was Cal, fed her the tender pot roast. Without seeing the food, the taste flooded her senses and she leaned back against Jackson.

"Hmmm, that tastes wonderful."

The next bite was a vegetable. Thelma always made certain the table had fresh vegetables out of the garden this time of year. She crunched on a green bean. Never before had she thought much about the texture and the taste of the beans, but today, she enjoyed every bite.

Everything seemed clearer.

She could hear Jackson crunching, so she knew he was also eating. When she wanted a drink she reached blindly for her glass and Jackson swatted her hands away.

"No, I'll get you your drink," he said.

A glass of water was brought to her lips and she drank.

"We should have had wine to celebrate," she said.

"No," Cal said. "We want you alert and aware of what is happening when we claim you."

"You're ours now," Jackson whispered against her ear. "Ours to take, to protect, and to cherish."

Warmth spread through her and she had no idea what was going to happen tonight, but she was ready. With these two men, she felt certain she'd found what she was searching for.

Next time the fork was filled with something sweet. Apples and then she felt Jackson's fingers caressing her center. For the next few minutes, they fed her and teased her until she was moaning. Finally, she heard Jackson set the fork down.

"Spread your legs," Cal said. "I'm going to shave you."

"What? Here at the table?"

The men chuckled.

"Why are you going to shave me?"

"The better to eat your cunt," Jackson whispered against her ear, sending a thrill through her.

Though she didn't quite understand what they were doing, she felt a brush swish across her lady parts, creating a sensation that left them tingling.

"Oh," she cried at the heat that engulfed her.

Then the razor scraped between her legs and she didn't dare move.

"Look at that sweet pussy," Cal said as she felt him wiping away the excess lather.

No, she couldn't see, but she knew enough about a

razor to understand the feel of the brush between her legs. Quivers spread through her body.

These were her men. Her husbands. And with them, she would experience so much desire. That she was certain of, since last night.

"Time to take this to the bedroom," Cal said. "You carry Bella and I'll bring dessert."

"I thought we had dessert?"

The men laughed. "Not yet."

Jackson helped her to stand and then he lifted her over his shoulder as he carried her up the stairs. They were going to her bedroom. Soon she would need to rearrange the house. Her parents' bedroom was much larger and it was on the ground floor.

This way their children could have the upstairs, if they stayed in Blessing. Funny, they had not discussed their plans yet. Did her men want to live here?

Right now, she had other things on her mind. Things that had her breathless with anticipation.

When they reached her room, Jackson's big, strong arms gently placed her on the bed. Nerves and anticipation prickled through her like the popping of a blazing campfire. Her breathing was harsh.

"Can I take the blindfold off?"

"Not yet," Jackson said.

The rustle of clothing came to her ears and she knew they were disrobing. She couldn't wait to experience them completely naked. Last night in the darkness, it had been hard to see. But tonight in the glow of the lanterns, she'd be able to see them. If they ever removed her blindfold.

She felt them sink onto the bed. One thing about being blindfolded was that she was more aware of sounds.

Each man grabbed one of her legs and spread her apart, their touches felt different. Cal's hands were not as large or rough as Jackson's and yet she enjoyed the feel of each man's touch. Would they feel different when they took her?

"Are you ready for dessert?" Jackson asked, his voice deep and low. The man was so handsome that even his voice had her pussy perking up, ready and waiting for him. Oh, how she wanted him.

"Yes," she said breathless at what they had planned.

Suddenly the feel of something cold and wet brushed against her pussy lips.

"Oh," she cried out as shimmers danced along her spine at the feel. "What is that?"

Then a mouth descended on her, sucking off the succulent juice, sending heat searing through her as she gasped at the feel of a tongue lapping at her folds.

"You're dessert," Cal said close to her ear. "Jackson is having whipped cream with your pussy."

Oh, how she wanted to look but knew better than to take off the blindfold. Her fingers reached for his head and grabbed onto his hair, holding him tightly. Needing him, she moaned as his tongue danced across her folds.

"Now for some dessert for you," Cal said.

She felt something on her lips and realized his cock was pushing into her mouth. What did he want her to do?

"That's right, sweetheart, let me in. Take my cock and let me give you your first lesson on sucking me," he said.

She realized there was cream on his manhood and she ran her tongue around the head licking it off, knowing instinctively this was what he wanted her to do.

He began to push it in farther and she opened her mouth wider to let him in. There was no way she could resist him and she really didn't want to. After all, Jackson was licking her folds and spiraling her closer and closer to the edge.

Fingers entered her pussy and she squeezed hard on the digits that manipulated her. Tensing, she could feel the orgasm building, creating tighter and tighter sensations, rushing her toward that cliff.

But would they let her come?

A second finger began to trail around the edge of her anus and while she wanted to tell him to stop, she couldn't. With a cock in her mouth and fingers in her pussy and soon to be ass, all she could do was try to hang on for the ride.

"Oh," she cried as the sensations twisted and twirled within her.

A moan escaped her and her hips rose to meet the fingers and mouth that were giving her so much pleasure.

"Come for me, baby," Jackson whispered. "Come now."

Cal pulled his cock from her mouth, still hard and in her face. When Jackson's finger sunk into her ass, she screamed her pleasure. A moan escaped as her body tensed and convulsed on his fingers.

"Please," she cried. "Fuck me."

Sitting on top of her, Cal reached down and kissed her,

his mouth tasting of whipped cream as she slowly came back down to earth.

His kiss was not gentle but demanding and he consumed her mouth, his tongue plunging inside, commanding her attention. Demanding and holding her close. She gave into his lips, knowing he would take all of her and she gladly surrendered.

Finally he released her mouth and she sighed, lying there spent, knowing they were not done for the night.

"Honey, Jackson, is going to break your maidenhead and then we'll both claim you."

"Yes, please, claim me, make me yours," she said, surprised at her words. But it was true. She was their wife. She wanted both her men.

Cal moved to the side of the bed and she felt something cold drop onto her nipples. She jerked at the feel of the liquid and knew they were once again making her their dessert.

The bed shifted and she knew Jackson was kneeling between her legs. With the blindfold still covering her eyes, she waited to feel his cock against her opening.

Slowly he rubbed his hard member up and down her slit, preparing her for his entry.

"I'm sorry, Bella, but the first time it's going to hurt just a little. But after that, the pleasure will be all ours," Jackson said.

"Do it," she cried, wanting the moment over and the pleasure to resume.

Cal's mouth covered her breasts as he licked up the whipped cream, his mouth sucking her nipple into his mouth. His teeth raking across her breasts. He tugged with his mouth, taking the nipple deep and she half rose off the bed at the sensation.

"Oh, Cal," she moaned.

Jackson pushed his cock into her and she could feel her body stretching to accept him. If her pussy was having a hard time taking him, how could her ass ever take him? She pushed the thought out of her mind, not wanting to dwell on that now.

With a deep breath, she prepared for his final surge and when it came, she felt the membrane break. "Oh, Jackson."

"Are you all right?" he asked as he paused.

"Yes, you're filling me up," she groaned as he waited for her body to accept his full length and width.

He seemed so big inside her.

Slowly he began to move, pushing and retreating, stroking and pulsating, as her pussy walls clenched his member. Leaning over her, he reached down and tweaked her clit, his fingers massaging the little button.

A groan escaped from her.

Once again, she was climbing the mountain reaching for the sun. Suddenly he stopped, holding her there.

"Take the blindfold off. I want to see her eyes when I claim our bride," Jackson said.

Cal removed it from her and she gazed up at her big strong man who made her feel like a beautiful woman. Who had secrets he wasn't sharing.

"You belong to us," he said to her, his body slowly

beginning to move once again. "Don't ever forget that we're your men. Say it."

"You're my men and I belong to you, only you," she said.

"When I say you can come, do it," he commanded as he moved within her.

This time he wasn't being hesitant. This time he was pounding into her pussy and she loved every minute. This time, she knew when she came, he would come to and she couldn't wait to experience the feel of his seed exploding inside her.

"Jackson," she cried. "I'm trying so hard to hold it back."

"Hold it," he said with a groan.

"Aargh, I can't," she said as the orgasm exploded inside her, lights shimmering behind her eyes as she rode the crest. Her body bucked and shuddered as she clenched around his cock, squeezing him, holding him inside her.

Just then she felt his seed hit the walls of her pussy and she knew he had also come as he gave her one last thrust, his cock buried deep inside her, his balls slamming against her pussy.

For a moment, all she could hear was heavy breathing as he slumped onto the bed. "You disobeyed."

"What?"

"You came without permission," he said, his breathing labored.

"It's because you're so good at what you do," she said, trying to help him understand that she couldn't hold back.

Yes, she had been a virgin, but still the feelings these two men evoked had her all but climbing the walls with need.

"Tonight, you only get three licks," Cal said. "And I'm going to give them."

"Will you spank my pussy?"

The two men turned and glanced at each other a smile on their face. "I think our wife enjoys her pussy being spanked."

Bella tilted her head and glanced up at them. "Is that bad?"

"Oh no, honey, we like it when you tell us what you want. What you like," Cal said. "Now crawl over my lap, so I can give you your punishment."

Bella sat up and then scooted across the bed to Cal. "Are you going to fuck me?"

"Of course. But we're going to do it in a different position. After I spank you, I want you up on your knees. I'm going to pound that sweet pussy of yours and spill my seed in you."

"What if I get pregnant?"

"We'll be the happiest two men in Blessing," Jackson said.

"But who will be the father?"

"Both of us," Cal replied. "Our children will all have a mother and two fathers. Now lie across my lap."

Bella did as she was told, tensing when she anticipated the first blow. But instead, Cal ran his hands over her ass cheeks, stroking them until she relaxed.

Slap!

She gasped at the sting.

"One," she said automatically falling into the same rhythm as the night before.

Slap!

"Two," she said, biting her lip, letting the burn spread through her straight to her pussy. Enjoying the heat that seemed to shimmer up her spine.

Slap!

"Three," she said and felt his fingers stroking her clit. She opened her legs, giving him more access wanting to feel the pleasure he evoked once again.

"Cal," she gasped.

"On your knees. I've waited too long. I'm about to explode."

Not knowing exactly what he was going to do, she got on her hands and knees. Just as she got into position, she felt a sting of pain and pleasure on her pussy as he slapped her there.

"Oh," she cried, the pleasure almost too much. "Do it again."

Smack. His hand landed on her pussy and she almost came.

"Open your mouth, Bella. I've been dreaming of you sucking my cock," Jackson said as he moved in front of her.

Licking her lips, she wrapped them around him and he groaned.

"Suck, baby, suck," he said.

She tightened her mouth around his large cock. Who would have dreamed that she would have two men satisfying her?

Suddenly she felt Cal slam his cock into her pussy and she moaned around Jackson's cock.

"Oh, do that again," Jackson said.

Cal slammed into her pussy pounding her, giving her his full length as he held her hips and rocked her back and forth to meet his needs. He was not gentle and she loved it, realizing she didn't want to be treated gentle in the bedroom, but rough.

His finger pushed into her ass and she groaned at the feel. She had a cock in her pussy, a finger in her ass, and a cock in her mouth. Two men who put her pleasure ahead of their own.

Tonight was their wedding night, but they had the rest of their lives to give each other pleasure. Already she knew she was falling for her men, giving them her heart and would do whatever it took to protect them. To love them.

"I'm going to come, honey, in your mouth. Swallow it all," Jackson said, leaning down close to her ear. His fingers reached down and twisted her nipples, causing fire to explode through her.

She moaned on his cock and that was all it took as Jackson grabbed her hair and held her to his cock as his seed exploded inside her mouth. It didn't taste bad, the essence reminded her of him.

Cal continued to pummel her pussy and when Jackson pulled back, she glanced over her shoulder at Cal and stared into his large brown eyes. She wanted to connect to his soul as he came. She wanted to watch him as he gave over to his orgasm.

"Cal," she groaned knowing she was close.

With another slam, his fingers reached between her legs and twisted her clit. "Come, Bella, come for me now."

And she did.

As she stared at him, she went to pieces, crying out her pleasure, screaming when he plunged once more into her pussy, shuddering and shaking and feeling certain that the house had just moved. Connecting with Cal in a way she never imagined.

All three of them collapsed onto the bed together. They placed her between them and she couldn't imagine a better place.

"How soon can we do this again?" she asked.

Her two men laughed.

"I think she's insatiable," Jackson said.

"Our perfect woman," Cal replied. "Soon, baby, soon."

11

Cal had never felt happier than he did this morning when he woke to Bella draped across his body. Though he only slept a few hours, he felt rested enough to want his new wife again.

As he held her, he gazed at her body and knew he would do whatever it took to protect her. His first wife he loved so very much until she died, leaving him devastated.

It wasn't until he met Jackson and they shared a prostitute that he considered the idea of sharing a woman. But now they had a wife and Cal couldn't wait to get her with child. He wanted children. A baby suckling at her breast. A toddler running through the house. Children playing outside.

Jackson stirred and rolled toward their woman.

"What a night," he said softly. "I don't think I've fucked that much since I was a young man."

Cal laughed. "This morning, we start her training."

The thought of them taking her together was enough to make him hard all over again. Yes, they would take it slow, but soon, she would be ready and willing.

"Let's wake her up," Jackson said as he laid his mouth over hers, consuming her lips as Cal watched.

His hand went down between her legs and he stroked her clit. Suddenly her eyes flew open and she moaned, wrapping her hands around Jackson's head, holding his mouth to hers.

Slowly, he broke the kiss.

"Good morning, my husbands," she said softly arching her back. "Didn't you get enough?"

"Never," Jackson said. "Roll over. Up on your elbows with your ass sticking up in the air."

Slowly she moved, her sapphire eyes glazed with passion.

Cal continued to stroke her, knowing they were preparing her for her first training.

"Every morning, we will awaken you with kisses and fucking. Every night we will put you to sleep with kisses and fucking."

"And you, my husbands," she said with a moan.

Jackson crawled out of the bed and a frown crossed her face. "Where are you going?"

"He'll be back," Cal said as he continued to stroke her clit, causing her to moan, wanting to shove his hard cock in her shorn pussy.

To distract her. He gazed into her eyes. "You're beautiful, Bella."

She started to disagree with him, but then she smiled. "Thank you."

They were making progress.

Jackson went to his saddle bags and pulled out the tools he needed. Cal thought it strange that he bought these at a shop in Fort Worth, not knowing when he would need them. And now they had a wife to use them on.

Grabbing a jar of ointment, Cal watched as Jackson spread it over the smallest of the plugs, preparing it for Bella.

Jackson crawled up on the bed behind her and spread her ass cheeks. Her head whipped around to him. "What are you doing?"

He held up the plug and showed it to her. "It's called a butt plug. It will prepare you to take both of us at the same time. This is the smallest one and when we reach the fourth, you will be ready for us."

Her mouth dropped open. "You're going to shove that in me?"

"Yes, sweetheart, I am. And I'll make certain you enjoy it."

Jackson rubbed some of the ointment on her puckered hole and then he began to push the pointed plug into her sphincter.

She tensed, and at Jackson's nod, Cal removed his hand from her clit. He reached down and slapped her on her pussy. "Relax, honey, it will go in easier."

A moan escaped her and Cal knew that when he popped her pussy, it increased her excitement, and like a flower, she slowly opened for Jackson.

"It's too big. How will I ever take one of you?"

"Soon, you will," Jackson said as he twisted the plug.

"Breathe, baby," Cal said, leaning down and gazing into her sapphire eyes. With his fingers on her clit, she began to move her hips and when she did, Jackson slipped the rest of the plug into her.

With a pop to her ass, he shoved his cock into her dripping pussy.

"Jackson," she cried. "I'm so full."

Cal leaned in again and pinched her nipples. "Just the way we want to fill you."

A moan escaped from her and she rocked back and forth with Jackson pumping into her. Already she gazed at him like a cat in heat. Like she wanted more.

"Oh, Jackson," she cried as he pummeled her pussy, his face tightening as he held onto her hips.

Cal couldn't wait until they both had her at the same time. Then he and Jackson would be fucking her and spilling their seed into her.

Twisting her nipples, her moans increased and he knew she was close.

"Jackson," she moaned.

He shoved into her wet pussy and slapped her ass. Just the sounds of their fucking were turning Cal so hard, he feared he would explode before he had the chance to experience her once again.

"Now you can come," Jackson groaned as he held her hips tightly and plunged into her soaking pussy.

A scream tore from her mouth as her body convulsed and she sank even farther onto the bed. "Ohhh."

Before she could come down completely from her climax, Cal took Jackson's position. Rising from the bed, he slipped behind her. Once again, he slapped her wet pussy, reigniting the nerves centered there and then plunged his cock into her.

"Cal," she screamed.

"Fuck me," he told her and she raised her ass higher allowing him to go deeper.

He thumped the plug in her ass and she moaned as he shoved his cock into her. Rough and not gentle, he gripped her hips, shoving into her cunty as he drove his cock home, pounding into her.

This was his woman, his wife, and he wanted his scent impaled upon her to drive other men away. Only with Jackson would he share her. She was theirs, and he felt this urge to mark her with his scent.

Much too soon, he could feel his seed building and knew it wouldn't be long before he came.

"Who do you belong to?" he gasped.

"You and Jackson," she moaned. "You're my men. My husbands."

"That's right and you better never forget it," he said as he popped her ass with his hand.

"Cal," she cried.

"Come for me, baby," he said as he pushed one last time into her cunt. "Come now."

With a scream, her body squeezed his cock, wringing every last drop of his come from him. She convulsed with the passion they created as he collapsed on top of her.

"Damn, Bella, I don't think I've ever experienced such great fucking before."

Jackson stroked her face as the three of them collapsed together in the bed with Bella between them.

Bella pulled them in close. "It was my lucky day when you found me."

12

Before breakfast, Cal looked at Jackson. "I think we should speak to the sheriff today."

"Good idea," Jackson said, knowing that the man had sent for them and the last couple of days they had been too busy with their new wife.

As they walked downstairs, they were surprised to see Bella had bathed, put on a fresh dress, and was now making them breakfast.

She turned and smiled at them and his heart clenched. Why the hell did he think he could fuck her and not have feelings grow for her? Who was he kidding? Already he could feel his heart reaching out to her, wanting, needing her love.

But he couldn't give it to her. No matter what.

"Are you hungry?" she asked.

"Yes," Cal said.

"Starving," Jackson replied. For her, not for the food. Sure, it was probably delicious, but he wanted to take her upstairs, strip that dress from her luscious body and sink his cock deep into her pussy.

Even after last night, he wasn't satisfied. Didn't know when he would get enough of this woman. But surely he could do this without falling in love with her. For some reason, it didn't feel possible.

Just thinking about it made his dick hard. Even after spending a night of sinking into her warm depths, he wanted more. And that frightened him.

She turned from the stove and set two plates of fried eggs and bacon on the table. Then she returned for hers.

This morning, his bride looked radiant. Her cheeks were flushed and her eyes were bright and sparkling even though they had very little sleep last night. And he doubted they would get much more tonight.

Cal held out her chair and helped her to sit.

"Are you wearing those bloomers women wear?" Jackson asked.

"Of course," she replied.

"Take them off, now," he said to her.

Her sapphire eyes widened and her mouth formed an O that he wanted to plunge his cock into. "Why?"

"Because I want to be able to lift your skirts and fuck you anytime I want."

A blush spread across his bride's face. "But what if we have visitors?"

"How will they know?" Cal said.

"What if the wind blows my skirt up?"

"You better be holding onto it dearly," Jackson said with a smile. The thought of his prim wife grabbing her skirt not to reveal her nakedness brought a chuckle to his lips.

"Better yet, just stay home," Cal said. "We don't want Lester anywhere near you."

"Are you leaving?"

"Honey, we were on our way to Blessing to take care of some local business. The sheriff sent for us," Jackson replied, knowing they had put off doing their job way longer than they planned.

"Just be waiting for us when we get home," Cal said. "Preferably with no clothes on."

"And don't answer the door to anyone," Jackson said. "I don't trust that guy Lester."

"Neither do I," Cal replied, finishing his plate. "And you're to leave the butt plug in place."

The sooner her ass was prepared for them the better. Already, Jackson wanted to sink his cock into her rosebud, knowing it would be tight.

Bella lifted her coffee mug. "I know. It just makes it hard to sit on certain surfaces."

"The more to remind you of how we're going to take you, both of us at the same time," Jackson said, knowing he couldn't wait.

"What case are you working on that caused you to come to here?"

For a moment, the men were silent, then Cal responded. "How many women have died here or in surrounding towns that were young and healthy?"

A frown crossed Bella's face. "At least three. Why?"

"The sheriff, who used to be a Texas Ranger, thinks a man is murdering women in this area. Someone who likes young, beautiful women. Another reason for you to stay home."

"I'm not—" Abruptly she broke off what she was going to say and glanced at both of the men.

"What were you going to say?" Cal asked. "It almost sounded like you were going to say something that would warrant you a spanking."

She bit her lip. "No, I stopped just in time."

"Did you take off your bloomers?"

Slowly she rose from the table, lifted her skirts and removed her bloomers giving them a flash of lovely bare pussy. Jackson stood and took them from her. "Now these are mine."

"Come here," Cal said.

She walked to him and he lifted her skirts and ran his hand over her cheeks and then swatted her ass.

"What was that for?"

"Because, darling, it was so tempting."

"Oh," she cried and he thumped the butt plug before he dropped her dress.

She smiled and before she could get back to her chair, Jackson pulled her down onto his lap. He liked the feel of her naked buttocks against his straining cock.

"Don't get dressed anymore," Cal said. "We want you available at all times."

Just the thought of her being naked beneath her skirts left Jackson hard and ready. But there was business that needed to be done.

"Did you know the women," Jackson asked, wondering if she could give them any clues.

"Greta Mason owned the restaurant before Lester. I don't know if he dated her, but he bought the cafe from her son. Really sad, because she was found in a ravine, brutally murdered. But they haven't found her killer yet. She was a really nice lady," Bella said, her sapphire eyes darkening with sadness.

"That must be why the sheriff sent for the Texas Rangers. He needs some help solving the murders."

Bella frowned. "I don't know anyone else that has been murdered."

"Did you know Martha Williams?"

"Oh yes, but she wasn't murdered. She left town."

"Her family says she never arrived in Dallas and her father said that jewelry was missing from her home. They think she's dead, but her body hasn't been found yet," Jackson said and couldn't help but sympathize with the family.

It was bad enough seeing your loved ones dead, but to not know what happened and for them to be missing, would be horrible.

"Oh, no, that's terrible," Bella said. "I hope she's all right. It would be awful for something to have happened to her."

Cal stood. "We need to get going, so we can get back here to you."

Bella smiled. "Yes, hurry home. I'll make sure dinner will be ready at five."

Jackson slid her off his lap, lifted her dress and cupped

her naked ass. "This is how I like my woman. Naked beneath her skirt."

A blush spread across her cheeks. "And I'm your woman."

"Yes, you are," he said. "After we leave, I want you to make certain the doors remain locked. Do not open the door to any man except me and Cal. Do you understand?"

"Yes."

"And do not leave the house. Stay home and wait for us."

Each man gave her a kiss as they walked to the door. All Jackson could think about was getting home to Bella.

13

Walking down the street, Cal thought the town of Blessing was a cute with all the necessary shops for people to survive, including a mercantile, bank, post office, telegraph office, sheriff, saloon, cafe, and even a tea parlor.

Crossing Main Street, they walked up the steps leading to the sheriff's office. Knocking, they entered. Seth Ingram rose from behind his desk where he was working.

"Good morning, gentleman. I see you survived the first nights of marriage."

"Cal is the husband," Jackson said.

The man smiled. "Gentlemen, I recognize two men in love with the same woman. Me and my friend Will Parker share my beautiful wife." Cal glanced at Jackson, his mouth dropping.

"It's a great arrangement and my wife loves us both," he said.

"Sorry, we didn't know there were others in this area," Jackson said.

"Oh, yes, Mack Savage and Jake Nash are married and share their wife Anna," the sheriff returned to his chair. "After you're settled, why don't we get together with the other husbands and wives."

Cal grinned. "That would be great."

Jackson sank down into a chair across from the sheriff. "So tell us what you know about the murders."

Seth leaned back and shook his head. "When the sheriff from Fredericksburg came over to talk about the murder in his town, everything started adding up."

"How so?" Cal asked.

"Ella Brown lived in Fredericksburg. She was murdered about six months ago. Strangled and stabbed over twenty times. A nice young woman, who was being courted by a new man in town, Jerry Smith."

Why were women so easily fooled by bad men? Even Bella was taken in by Lester and that man looked ruthless.

"At the time, Martha Williams's family had come to town looking for her. We discovered her jewelry missing and some other valuable items. But we have not found a body. Plus, I'm still trying to figure out who killed Greta Mason. Poor Greta suffered the same fate as Ella Brown. Strangled with multiple stab wounds."

Cal didn't like the sound of any of this. Two dead women and one missing, presumed to be dead.

"Have you checked with the sheriffs in other towns around here?" Jackson asked.

"Yes, I'm waiting to hear back from them."

"How long between the murders?" Cal asked, thinking he needed to know the time frame the man committed these crimes. Especially if he was courting women. That would take some time.

"Ella Brown was six months ago. Greta Mason about eight months ago and Martha Williams disappeared three months ago."

The three of them all stared at one another.

"This seems way too coincidental. Every two to three months a woman is being killed. It's been three months. If we have a murderer living amongst us, he is due to strike just any time," Cal said.

Seth nodded. "And that's why I contacted the Texas Rangers. I thought maybe together we could catch this bastard before he killed anyone else."

"Was Martha seeing anyone new?" Jackson asked.

Cal waited, thinking of the chances that each woman was being courted by a new man, who just happened to disappear when he learned of her death. Something wasn't right.

"Not that I know of, but her family received an urgent telegram from her saying she was coming home. She was our school teacher here in town and she quit in the middle of the school year. Not many teachers do that."

No, they didn't. It was odd that she would suddenly want to leave town unless she was being threatened.

"What about close friends? Anyone who can tell us why she left in a hurry?" Jackson asked.

Cal always depended on Jackson. The man was smart

when it came to investigating people. He trusted his opinion.

"Not that I know of, but I'll ask my wife," Seth said.

"And we'll ask ours. She believed Martha had just left town. She didn't know she was missing."

Cal sat there contemplating how they could stop this killer. "How many single women are in town?"

Seth shrugged. "I have no idea. In a small town, you wouldn't think there would be many."

Jackson stood and began to pace the floor. "We need to warn them. Get all the single ladies together and tell them that we fear for their lives. Learn if any of them are seeing a new man."

"Won't that scare them?" Cal asked, knowing he didn't want to frighten the ladies, but he did want to catch this killer.

"Probably, but I'd rather they were alive and frightened than dead," Jackson said. "We'll talk to our wives and see if we can gather a list. I bet the pastor at the church would also know how many single women are in town."

Seth nodded. "I like this idea. But we need to hurry. I'll get posters made to tell the women to come to the church and we'll tell them there. We'll do it early one evening and ask that the women let us escort them home."

Jackson nodded.

Cal agreed, but he didn't like the idea of the ladies' homes being empty while they were gone. He would insist on a man escorting them home and checking out their house. Already, three women had lost their life; they didn't want to lose any others.

Now to determine how many single women lived here and if they were alone. Maybe they could talk some of the widows into staying with the ladies. Anything to save these women from this killer.

"In the meantime, we'll talk to our wives and see if they can tell us who might know why Martha Williams was leaving town, who the single ladies are, and come together tomorrow. It would be great if we could meet the ladies tomorrow evening."

Seth stood. "Sounds like a good plan. That's why I called you to come."

"And thank you for that," Cal said with a smile. "We would not have married Bella if not for coming to visit."

A frown crossed his face. "We need to talk to her about Lester. Maybe we should be looking into the single men in this town as well. Learn who is dating the women."

"You're welcome. And I never understood what she saw in Lester. In fact, do you know what he said that made her run?"

"She overheard him call her ugly and he wanted her for nothing but her bank account."

The sheriff frowned. "Bella seems like an extremely smart woman and she was scared of Lester. My gut is telling me it's more than just words. See what you can find out."

A frown crossed Cal's face. Seth was right. What sent his wife galloping across the hot prairie that day? There was something she wasn't telling them.

"I'm happy to know that you two are making her happy. Bella deserves all the happiness in the world."

They grinned at one another. "And she's making us very happy. Now if you'll excuse us, Sheriff, it's almost supper time and we should go home and check on our woman and ask her some questions."

"Questions, my ass," Seth said with a smile. "I know what you're going to be doing with your woman. Enjoy, because once the first baby arrives, things change."

"We can't wait," Cal said and they walked out the door.

14

Bella had given the housekeeper the week off. For a while, she didn't want anyone in the house hearing what was going on behind closed doors. Last night, her screams of passion were probably enough to wake the neighbors.

She gazed around the kitchen, wondering what to create for dinner. They were big, strong, hungry men who needed nourishment to keep up their strength.

They were out of milk and eggs. While her men had told her not to leave the house, she only needed to go up a block to the mercantile. She would be back before they knew she was gone. Besides, she was used to doing what she wanted.

What harm would it cause for her to go to the mercantile?

Grabbing her umbrella, she left the house and raced down the street avoiding eye contact, wanting to hurry.

Once inside the mercantile, she grabbed the milk and eggs and hurried to the counter.

"Congratulations on your marriage, Bella," Mr. Bailey said. He handed her a piece of chocolate. "A little wedding gift to share with your husband."

"Why thank you," Bella said, knowing that the man was the most chintzy person in town and for him to give her a nickel worth of chocolate was a big deal.

"Is your husband going to stay here in town? I heard he was a Texas Ranger."

Stunned, she realized they had not discussed their plans and she had assumed they would remain here in Blessing. What if they asked her to leave? Would she go with them?

"We'll see," she said. "We're not making any decisions until he finishes the case he's on."

"Case?"

She realized she probably shouldn't have said anything. Jackson and Cal might not want the town knowing they were investigating a murder.

"It's not big," she said, picking up her items and heading toward the door.

"Congratulations," he called. "Tell them I said hello."

She halted when Lester walked in the door. He stood there grinning at her, like he was waiting for her. Eager to taunt her. But she would not take the bait, she wouldn't.

"Where are your Texas Rangers?" he said in a sneering voice. "I don't see them here to protect you."

Like a snake, fear wrapped around her chest, squeezing

her heart. She took a deep breath, determined not to let this man intimidate her any longer.

"Why would I need protecting from you. Now move out of my way," she demanded.

"No, you're leaving with me," he said. "We're going on that fancy honeymoon I promised you."

There was no honeymoon planned. They were going to return to her home. Today, Bella realized that the man had not paid anything for their wedding. She had footed all the bills and she realized her marriage would be the same way.

"I'm not going anywhere with you," she replied. "Mr. Bailey, would you get the sheriff?"

Lester growled at the man and pulled a gun. "Don't move, Bailey, unless you want a bullet in you. I'm not in any kind of mood to hesitate today. This woman has made me look like an ass."

"That's because you are," Bella said softly.

"Lester, she's married to a Texas Ranger. Be smart, leave her be," he said. "If they catch you, you'll be a dead man."

Bella had to get out of here before Lester did something stupid that would anger her men. They would not be happy that she had gone to the mercantile and risked putting herself in danger.

At the time, it seemed so innocent and yet now she was in trouble.

Serious trouble.

The man's face was red as he walked toward her and fear scurried down her spine. How had she ever considered him to be her husband. He didn't love her and he didn't find her beautiful. And she no longer thought he was even worth considering.

"You're such an ugly woman. Look at you. Your blonde hair isn't full and curly. You have a long nose and your hips are way too large. I'm glad I didn't marry you because you're ugly."

Tears welled up in her eyes and she tried not to listen to him. Her men assured her she was beautiful. And oh, how she wanted to believe them, but when she looked in the mirror, she saw everything that Lester was saying.

"You only wanted to marry me for my money," she said, ignoring his comments.

He laughed. "Why do I need your money. I have the restaurant and soon I'm going to build a hotel."

"Then if you found me ugly, why were you marrying me, if not for my inheritance?"

"Because I thought with your decorating skills, you would be good in the hotel business. But instead you made me into a laughing stock in town. You humiliated me."

Bella took a step back and another one. If only she could get around him, she would run out the door, but he was closing in fast on her. Why had she left the house? Why had she come here without her husbands?

"I'm a good mind to fuck you right here in front of Mr. Bailey. I waited for you and now you gave your maidenhead to a man you didn't even know. You're a whore."

His words frightened her and made her angry. If she got out of here, she would never leave the house alone again. She would wait for her men.

"My husband is more man than you will ever be. I was

lucky to get out of marrying you. God was watching over me when I overheard you tell your friend you only wanted my money and that you were going to kill me."

He grinned at her. "It was all talk. Nothing more."

"You said you would only have to fuck me once," she said.

"You're right, I did say that. You're too ugly to fuck more than once," he said, laughing as he reached for her.

Oh, how she wanted to throw it in his face that her husbands had fucked her many, many times just last night, but she couldn't tarnish their names by throwing it at this evil man.

Suddenly he was right in front of her reaching out to grab her arm.

She smashed the jar of milk over his head, cracking it into pieces. For a moment, he was stunned and she ran around him and out the door, straight into the arms of her husbands.

15

Cal's arms reached out and grabbed her. "Damn it, Bella we told you not to leave the house."

Something was wrong. She looked terrified. Jackson could see the fear in her sapphire eyes and knew someone had threatened her, but who?

He stepped into the mercantile and saw Lester with milk running down his face, glass all over the floor. Mr. Bailey stood behind the counter, his face white.

"Thank God you're here," Bailey said.

"What happened?" Jackson asked.

"He said some vicious things to your wife. Horrible and I think he would have harmed her, except she broke the milk jar over his head and ran out. I was going to fetch the sheriff, but he threatened to shoot me. Get him out of my store, and Lester don't come back."

The man seemed to come to life then and he growled. "Your store is a garbage pit. Don't worry, I won't be back."

The jerk moved to walk past Jackson like he thought

he was going to get away with scaring Bella, but that wasn't going to happen. Jackson reached out and grabbed the front of Lester's shirt and pulled him in close. "You touch Cal's wife and you're a dead man. Do you understand me?"

"I don't want that whore," he said.

Because he was a lawman was the only reason he got away with calling Bella that word. But there were other ways to get to him. With one hand on his shirt, he grabbed the man's belt and yanked his pants as high as he could.

"Aargh, you're hurting me."

"Never call Mrs. Thomas a whore. Do you understand? Or next time your pants will be up around your neck and your balls will hang there."

"Stop," Lester croaked.

"Now someone frightened her and I think it was you. Don't be frightening Mrs. Thomas again. In fact, if she's walking down the street, you better cross to the other side. If I hear of you getting near her again, I will beat you until you wished you were dead. And your cock will be useless. Do you understand?"

"Yes," he choked.

Jackson released the man and gave him a shove. "Now get the hell out of my sight before I lose control and give you that beating now."

"We're not done by any means," Lester said almost doubling over. "And Bailey, I'm going to put you out of business."

The man yanked his pants down and straightened his shirt before he hurried out the door. Good riddance.

When Jackson walked back outside, Cal was glaring at Lester. "Did he try to hurt you?"

"No, I hurt him," she said. "I broke the milk jar over his head."

"And I raised his pants until he was talking like a girl," Jackson said.

Cal grinned at him. He knew what he'd done to the man. And Jackson knew he approved.

"Let's get you home," Jackson said. "I've taken care of Lester. If he bothers you again, he's a dead man."

She seemed to sag in Cal's arms. "I'm so sorry. You told me not to leave the house, but we needed milk and eggs and I didn't think it would hurt to go to the store. It was fine until he walked in."

Cal frowned down at her. "How long were you in the store before he appeared?"

"Just long enough to get the eggs and milk. I paid for them and was about to walk out when he came through the door."

Jackson glanced at Cal and growled. The man was waiting for her.

"I don't think that was a coincidence. He was watching you," Cal said.

Furious, Jackson took her by the arm and so did Cal. She had disobeyed them and she would be punished.

"Bailey told me he said some horrible things to you. What did he say?" Jackson asked, his temper razor thin from losing control.

Tears sprang into her eyes and she sniffed. "If I tell you, you'll kill him."

"No, he's going to have to do more than just say words. I might beat the shit out of him, but he'll live," Jackson promised.

She gazed at him, worry filling her sapphire eyes. "He said I was ugly. My hair isn't full and curly. I have a long nose and my hips are way too large. He was glad he didn't marry me, because I'm ugly."

"That fucker needs glasses," Cal said. "Now I may kill him."

"Tell me what we say to you all the time," Jackson said, stopping on the street and turning her toward him. "Tell me."

"You tell me I'm beautiful. But he's right. When I look in the mirror, all I see is my long nose and straight hair and my hips have always been large."

Cal spun her to face him. "You're going to be punished when we get home for going out, but when we tell you you're beautiful, we mean it. We're not lying. We love your hair. Your nose is cute and perky and your hips, dear God, are just right for grabbing onto and holding you while we fuck you. His words were meant to belittle and hurt you. Don't let him win."

"Say it," Jackson said as he whirled her to face him. "I want you to tell me what I need to hear."

"I'm beautiful," she said softly.

"You're damn right you are," Cal said.

"Those sapphire eyes make me hard every time and that long nose is fun to kiss. As for your hips, oh hell yes, I like to hold onto them while I shove my cock in you."

A sob escaped from her and Jackson realized she was

crying. He wanted to take her in his arms and comfort her, but they were standing on the streets of Blessing. Anyone could see them.

"This is why you're my husbands," she said softly. "Thank you."

"Let's go home," he told Cal. "It's getting late and we have much to discuss. A spanking to give and then I'm going to spread her legs and shove my cock in as far as it will go."

"Baby, you should not have left the house," Cal said.

"I know that now, but I'm used to doing things when I want and I thought I'd be right back."

People on the street were turning and glancing at them. Jackson wanted to get home, where they could fix this problem in a hurry.

"Time to go," he said, taking her by the arm. Cal took the other arm and they walked the short block to her house.

Tonight, it would be Cal spanking her. Jackson took a deep breath. Lester could have taken her away from them. He could have hurt her, and even a worse thought came to mind: what if he were the killer?

Jackson could have lost her just like he had his family.

16

When they walked into the house, she knew they were going to punish her. Part of her knew they were right, but she honestly didn't think she would be in any danger. How many times had she gone to the mercantile and never once experienced what she did today?

"Go upstairs, take off your clothes, get into position and wait for us," Cal said.

"I agree. I disobeyed you and I shouldn't have," she said, fear causing her hands to clench. "But I didn't think it would be dangerous."

Jackson scowled at her. "Get upstairs."

A sigh escaped her, as with a flounce, she turned and headed up the stairs to her bedroom. Meeting up with Lester had been terrifying, but she didn't expect to see him today. The thought of him following or waiting for her sent a shiver through her.

No, she wouldn't disobey again. She had learned her lesson.

In the background, she could hear them talking.

As she removed her clothes, she worried about how hard they would be spanking her, because she was certain she would be punished.

Soon she heard their footsteps on the wooden stairs and made certain she was in the position they wanted, with her head down on the bed, ass in the air.

When they came into the room, she was tempted to glance back at them, but then thought better. Right now, any little thing would give her more licks.

She felt Cal's hand helping her up off the bed. "Across my lap, Bella."

A tear streamed down her face. What more could go wrong today? She laid across his lap, her long blonde hair falling to the floor.

"Bella, the reason for your punishment is because we came home to an empty house. There was nothing telling us where you were. You frightened us. Because we didn't know if you had been taken or if you had gone to see someone," Jackson said.

Cal rubbed her buttocks in a stroking manner and she knew no matter what she said, she would be punished tonight.

"And we expressly told you not to leave the house. We meant what we said," Cal told her. "You disobeyed and for that you're going to receive five hard licks."

Splat!

The force surprised her and she squirmed on Cal's lap trying to get comfortable, knowing these licks were going to be painful.

"One," she said resigned to her fate. They would make certain she didn't forget this spanking. They would make certain that she thought twice about disobeying them.

Splat!

"Two," she said, determined not to cry, though already she'd been crying. But she didn't want them to know how the punishment spankings were much worse than the other times they spanked her. These hurt.

Splat!

"Three," she groaned, wondering how much more she could take.

The third one almost sent her over the edge and tears rolled down her face into her hair.

Splat!

"Four. Please no more," she cried moving on his leg, anything to stop the stinging on her buttocks.

Splat!

"Five," she screamed, crying and trying to get away from him. She didn't want another one.

Her ass felt like it was on fire. It burned and ached and she knew it would be sore the next day.

Cal pulled her up and into his arms. "For your safety, you must obey us. We're your husbands and we will protect you with our life, but you've got to listen to us."

"I didn't think it would hurt to go to the mercantile," she said, sniffing leaning against him.

Jackson rubbed her back, his hands trying to reach her buttocks to rub her sore, aching, muscles.

"We would have gladly gone to the store with you

when we got home," Jackson told her. "Then I could have pounded that jerk when he talked bad about you."

Cal held her and rubbed and soothed her as he stroked her back. "Wait for us and we'll take you wherever you want to go."

Several minutes later, Cal laid her on her back on the bed. "Spread your legs, baby, and let me make you feel better."

Her husband moved between her legs and spread her wide. She watched as his mouth descended onto her clit, sucking it into his mouth, sending pleasure cascading through her.

Jackson moved to the head of the bed and leaned over her. "Open your mouth, Bella, and suck my cock."

The man was bigger than Cal, but she managed to get her lips around his manhood and she licked the head of his bulbous organ, knowing he would soon come in her mouth.

The butt plug remained in her ass and she felt Cal pull it out, twist it and shove it back in. Strange, but it made her feel full. The movement sent shocks of pleasure spiraling through her. And she wondered how her husbands would feel in her backside. Would she enjoy their cocks there?

Jackson pulled his member out of her mouth.

"Cal, please," she groaned as his fingers continued to tweak her clit, rubbing over the folds between her legs, stroking her and occasionally shoving his fingers inside her pussy. The man was driving her crazy with his fingers and she wanted his cock.

"What do you want?" he asked.

"You," she whispered. "Your cock."

He obliged her, shoving the hard member in as she clenched it with her muscles. The movement soothed the ache that was building inside her. It grounded her and made her want him even more. She wanted him deeper as she gritted her teeth, her muscles straining to hold him.

"Yes, baby, do that again," he groaned and she smiled knowing she pleased him.

Jackson plunged his dick back into her mouth and she continued to suck on his hardened manhood.

"Bella, you're beautiful all splayed out here for us. Your mouth on Jackson, me shoving my cock in your pussy. You are the most beautiful woman and you belong to us."

He plunged his cock inside her and she groaned around Jackson while she clenched Cal with the walls of her pussy.

While she hated her punishment and the guilt of how she had disobeyed, now they were making her feel wonderful. Reminding her of how beautiful they thought her. Giving her pleasure and telling her she belonged to them. Only them.

And she wanted no one else.

Again, Cal twisted the butt plug, pulling it out and pushing it back in her in rhythm with his cock. A fullness, she never thought to experience consumed her, and every time he twisted it, she wanted more.

"I'm going to come," Jackson said and she felt his explosion of seed hit the back of her throat.

"You can come anytime," Cal told her and she could feel that he was close.

Jackson pulled his cock from her mouth as she swallowed his essence. He reached down and pulled at her nipples and that was enough to send her over the edge.

With a scream, she squeezed Cal's cock and felt him flood her pussy with his seed as he pulsated within her.

"Oh," she cried out, knowing her husbands had changed her life for the better and she wanted to do nothing but please them. Make them happy.

As her orgasm ended, she glanced at her two men, thankful for them.

For a moment, they lay there catching their breath, floating, enjoying the glow of the experience.

"Get the next plug, she's ready," Cal said.

Jackson slowly rose from the bed and strode over to Cal's saddle bags where he pulled the next size up. In a haze of pleasure, she watched him cover it with a lubrication.

Was she ready for the next size? That one looked even larger.

"On your hands and knees, Bella," Jackson said. "Only a couple of more of these, before we can both take you."

Slowly she rolled to her knees and he removed the previous plug. Massaging her buttocks, Jackson began to insert the new size. It didn't hurt as much as the first one, but she could feel her body stretching to accommodate the larger size.

When it was completely in, he gave her a gentle swat to the butt.

"Get dressed. We need to talk," he said.

She glanced back at him and could see he had something serious he wanted to discuss.

17

Jackson had that serious look about him. The one that was all business. While Bella cleaned up and put on a robe, they went downstairs and fixed a pot of coffee.

While they watched the sun go down, they sat around Bella's table, waiting for her to appear.

"Why would Lester be waiting on Bella to come out unless he meant to harm her?" Jackson said. "I've thought about this since she said he came into the mercantile not long after she arrived."

"Do you think he's our murderer? He did threaten to kill Bella. At the time, I thought it was talk, but now I'm not certain."

They were silent for a few moments as Cal went over everything in his mind. All the clues, the women, everything.

Finally, Jackson sighed. "Don't know for certain he's the one we're after. But if we jump to conclusions, we could miss the real killer and he was involved with two of the women."

A frown crossed Jackson's face. "Do we know if he has ever been married? Have we checked into his background at all?"

"No," Cal said, thinking this was why they worked so well together. Jackson was probably the smartest man he knew.

"Tomorrow, let's see if we can learn where he came from and send a telegram to the law enforcement in that town."

Just then they heard Bella coming down the stairs. Cal stared at her in the robe, her face was flushed, her eyes bright, and she was the most gorgeous woman he'd ever met. His heart sped up just gazing at her.

"Sit down," Cal said. "Do you want some coffee?"

"No," she said, gazing at them. "What's going on?"

Cal reached out and took her hand in his. Jackson did the same.

"You know we're here investigating a murder."

"Yes," she said, her expression one of confusion.

"We want to talk to all the single women in town at once. After meeting with the sheriff, we think that the killer may be getting ready to kill again. He seems to kill about every two months."

Bella gasped, her eyes widening. "You're afraid he's going to kill another woman in town."

"Yes, so we thought if you knew the single ladies, you could tell us their names and we'd like to meet with them tomorrow night. Warn them to be careful. Not to go out courting because we don't have a clue to who this killer is."

Shaking her head, Bella sighed and visibly relaxed. "When you said you wanted to talk, I was afraid you were going to tell me we were done."

Stunned, Cal stared at her. "Are you kidding? You're not getting rid of us that easy."

Did she have so little confidence in them that she thought they would leave her? Then he remembered the words that Lester had flung at her.

"Honey, we're yours until death do us part," Jackson said, reaching out and stroking her face.

A smile crossed her face and she sighed. "I'm so glad. Now let me get a piece of paper and a pencil. I'll tell you all the single ladies in town. There are only about eight right now that I know of."

Cal nodded, feeling better about warning the women already. They didn't know when the killer would strike again, but they would do everything they could to stop him.

"Do you think Lester could be the killer?" Jackson asked her.

Immediately she sighed. "I don't know. When I was sitting in the bride's room at church, waiting for the ceremony to begin, I overheard him and his friend. He mentioned killing me. Until now, I never really thought about it seriously, especially since he was drunk."

A trickle of alarm went down Cal's spine. That was brazen. To tell a friend you intended to kill your bride was just cold. Even if he were only joking, it was mean.

"What's the name of the friend?" Jackson asked.

"Randal Jones. He did work in the saloon," she said. How could she have gotten to the point of agreeing to marry Lester? A shiver traveled down her spine. She'd been lucky to escape.

"Why didn't you tell us this?" Cal asked, wondering why she kept this to herself.

"I was stunned. And when I thought about it later, I wondered if I had truly heard what he said. It didn't seem real."

Cal shook his head. "But we told you about the murders. Why didn't you mention it then?"

"Again, I didn't believe that it was him. He was drunk that morning. All kinds of things were spewed from his lips."

"We're going to speak to Randal tomorrow as well," Cal said.

Jackson took a big drink of his coffee and Cal knew him well enough to know that something was troubling him. When he set the drink down, he glanced at Cal and then turned his attention to Bella.

"Do you think the women in Blessing will take heed if we warn them?"

"Yes, I do. Maybe not the girls at the saloon, but everyone else will. What about that teacher? Did you learn anything more about her?"

Cal bit his lip. The woman was dead. He was almost certain. They just hadn't found her body yet and he worried they never would.

"Is there anyone else in town, any new men, anyone at all who you think would kill these girls?"

Bella thought about it for a moment. "No. We're a small peaceful town. We've had some trouble with stagecoach robbers, but that was because of the banker and the owner of the whorehouse. One of the ranchers was a troublemaker, but he's dead now."

Something about this Lester character screamed out that he was the man they were searching for, but they didn't have any proof. Just hearing that he said he would kill Bella didn't amount to anything. It was nothing they could charge him with.

They needed hard evidence.

"Will you help us tomorrow night to get the women to attend the meeting?" Jackson asked.

"Of course," she said. "Any other questions?"

"No, I think you've answered them all," Jackson said.

"Good, now take me back upstairs and let's finish what you started tonight. Only, please don't spank me hard again."

Both men grinned and Jackson picked her up and threw her over his shoulder.

"With pleasure, ma'am," he said in that low voice drawl that all the women adored.

Cal followed him up the stairs. This woman was capturing his heart. Already he could feel his emotions becoming entangled with her and he felt frightened that something would happen to her.

They had to protect her at all costs. Especially from Lester.

18

Cal stood before the small group of women inside the church where he had married Bella. With the names from his wife and Seth's wife, they had contacted nine women. Only seven showed up in the church chapel.

"Thank you for coming, ladies," Cal said, gazing out at the group sitting on pews. In the back was the pastor and he watched the proceedings with interest.

Somehow he had to warn these women without frightening them to death. But there was a danger and he wanted them to be prepared.

"We know you must be wondering why Texas Rangers are here in Blessing and wanting to talk to single women."

The women smiled at him. A week ago, he would have been trying to figure out which one to try to seduce, but now he glanced at his wife in the back of the room and knew no one else mattered but her.

All he wanted to do was save these women from the monster out there who was killing women.

"Let me tell you what the sheriff and the Rangers are concerned about."

For the next ten minutes, he explained how each woman had either been killed or went missing here in Blessing and also in Fredericksburg. Their faces went from disinterested to alarmed, and they were now hanging on his every word.

"Do you have any suspects," one lady asked.

"Not really. We have some people we're checking into, but no one we would name," he said. "In fact, I was wondering if any of you ladies know of someone who would be capable of killing women."

Sometimes women were afraid to go to the law when someone either attacked them or intimidated them. Here was their chance to help them find this killer.

They all shook their head. Finally a woman spoke up. "Jim Lankford drinks too much and has a mean temper, but I don't think he would kill anyone."

"Anyone else?"

The women begin to give names of who they should check. Finally at the last moment, a very mousy woman stood. He could see that she was having trouble speaking. Her hands shook and she clenched them in front of her.

"Have you checked Lester Clark?" Tears sprang to her eyes and she sniffed. "He tried to rape me."

The room went silent and then Bella went to her side and hugged her. "Honey, are you all right?"

"Yes, I always carry a small pocket knife and I stabbed him in the arm with it. I've never been so scared in all my life."

"Thank goodness," Bella said, giving the woman encouragement. "I remember when he had a wound on his arm. That was while he was courting me."

She nodded. "That's why I was so surprised. My papa always said it's the ones you least expect."

Bella hugged her again. "I'm so sorry this happened to you."

Cal was ready to arrest the creep right now. To hell with gathering evidence, just arrest him and haul him to jail. But he knew in order to keep him in jail, he would need to prove he was their killer.

Somehow Lester had just become their prime suspect. All because this woman had the courage to stand up and admit she survived an attack. She was a little woman and Cal couldn't imagine her fighting off a big man.

"Why didn't you report it the sheriff?" Cal asked, needing to hear her answer.

"Why? He wasn't successful and now I avoid him at all costs."

It was true. What could the sheriff do?

"Does anyone know anything about Lester?" Jackson asked. "We'd like to find out more about him."

An older woman, a widow stood. "Yes, he was married once. Lived in Boston until he decided to come out west. The only reason I know is because I'm from Boston. We talked about living there."

"Thank you," Jackson said.

This was exactly the information Jackson was after. In the morning, they would send a telegram to the law enforcement in Boston asking about Lester, trying to find out if he had committed any crimes there.

"Thank you," Cal said. "Anything else that you want to tell us?"

"Kill the son of a bitch," the older widow woman said.

The women giggled, but no one else said anything.

"Ladies, we don't want you walking home alone, so we're going to escort you to your homes tonight."

Just then the door to the church opened and Seth Ingram ran in, his face white. Cal took one look at him and knew something was terribly wrong. Either someone else had died or they found a body.

"What's happened?"

"We just found Lillian Rodriquez's body in a ditch about three miles from town. She was strangled and stabbed multiple times just like the others."

Cal clenched his fists, his anger rising inside him. He wanted to curse, but held back, not wanting to insult the women. Another body.

The women gasped. "She worked at the saloon."

"Yes," the sheriff replied. "She worked last night."

That meant the killer had either taken her today or late last night after she got off work.

"What can we do to help?" Jackson asked the sheriff.

"Help me at the crime scene to make certain I've not overlooked something. But I thought you and the ladies needed to hear and understand, we have a killer living among us."

Bella's eyes grew wide. "It's dark. How can you work the investigation now?"

Cal knew she didn't want to be alone tonight. Not with some man here in town killing women.

"We covered and protected the body as best we could. We'll return in the morning. In the meantime, ladies, do not go out alone at night. I don't want to find any of your bodies," Seth said as he gazed at the ladies in church.

Jackson nodded. "We'll escort these ladies home, and first thing in the morning, we'll go with you to where you found the body."

The ladies all stood and suddenly the widow woman grabbed several of their hands. "I think since we're in church, we should say a prayer for Lillian and ask God to help us find this murderer."

The other women nodded and the ladies bowed their heads and asked for God to protect them and heal the pain Lillian's family would go through. It was a sweet prayer and Cal nodded his approval.

When it was over, they begin to divide the women into groups to escort home. Each lawman took two to three women.

"Let's get you ladies home," Jackson said as he walked the women out the door.

19

Jackson stared at the body of Lillian Rodriquez. The woman had been stabbed multiple times and there were bruise marks around her throat.

As he stared at the half naked body, fear seized his chest. He'd seen the bodies of his family and sworn never to love again, and yet, he could feel his heart becoming involved with Bella. What if this had been her body? What if the killer got to her?

He wanted to give her his love, but he was so afraid of losing someone he cared about again. It would devastate him and he didn't know if he would continue on.

"This is one sick son of a bitch," Cal said, gazing at the woman. "It appears he raped her. Look at the bruise marks on her thighs. This was not a consensual joining."

Rage consumed Jackson. No woman should have to endure this kind of death. And yet he had now killed three women and a fourth was missing. They had to find this bastard.

"Are there rope marks around her wrists?" Cal asked.

"Yes," Seth said, lifting her arm as he shook his head. "I'd kill anyone who did this to someone I loved."

"Agreed," Cal said. "We've got to find him before he does this again, because he will kill again."

Jackson had killed before, but only because he was forced to as a law officer. Never for pleasure and never a woman. What this man had done left him nauseous and filled with anger.

"Let's review the victims," Jackson said.

"Greta Mason, the owner of the cafe. Stabbed multiple times and was dating Lester. Does he have an alibi for that night?"

Seth frowned. "Said he was at the saloon that night and his friend Randal verified he was there with him."

"Was there anything about her murder that was different from this woman?"

Seth frowned. "I don't think she was raped. Brutally stabbed and even strangled, but I don't remember seeing dried semen or bruises on her legs. Not like Lillian."

"What about Ella Brown?" Jackson asked, needing to go over the victims murders just in case there was something they missed.

"I didn't see her body. The sheriff came over and told me about her murder. I do know she was stabbed and strangled. They found her nude body in a field outside of town."

All the women had been dumped outside of town. So why hadn't they found Martha Williams's body? Had she just disappeared or was she murdered.

"Martha Williams is still missing and now we have Lillian Rodriquez to include with the victims. What did Miss Rodriquez do for a living?"

Shaking his head, Seth frowned. "I don't really know. But she liked to hang out at the saloon."

Not many ladies hung out at a saloon. So obviously, the woman didn't have a great reputation, but still she didn't deserve to die this way.

"Could she have been a whore?"

"Don't know," Seth said. "I need to speak to the saloon owner and see what he can tell me."

Jackson nodded. "By the way, one of the women last night told us that Lester was from Boston. They had spoken about their commonality. We sent a telegram to law enforcement to see if they could tell us anything about him."

"Great idea," Seth said.

Big black birds swarmed overhead. One thing about being out in the open, the earth had a way of dealing with the remains. So where was the other woman?

"What are you going to do with the body?" Cal asked, still staring at the woman who lay at an odd angle in the ditch. Her body almost appeared to have been shoved off a horse.

Such disrespect for any human was ungodly, but especially a woman.

"The undertaker is coming. I'm going to meet him here. Why don't you two go back into town and speak to the saloon owner. Maybe he can tell us who she was with last night."

Cal sighed. "Gruesome sight. Who are her family?"

"Don't know," Seth said. "Ask the saloon owner. As far as I know, she was all alone here in Blessing."

Jackson walked over to his horse. A sight like this always brought the memory of his family murders back and tonight he would probably have nightmares, go over their murders in his dreams once again. See their bodies and feel the pain again.

He climbed into the saddle. "Let's go. I've seen enough."

Cal climbed onto his mare. "Agree. I've seen way more than I ever wanted to."

It took them about thirty minutes to ride back into town. The first place they went by was the saloon. They tied their horses to the hitching post and went in.

"Who owns this place," Jackson asked a bar maid. Even though it was early afternoon, there were men and even a few ladies in the darkened room.

She smiled at him like she wanted to eat him for supper, but Jackson was not interested in what she had to offer. He had a wife at home that he was trying to protect from a killer in town. To spare other families from receiving a message from the sheriff that their daughter was dead. Murdered.

"George Martin. He's behind the bar," she said, winking at him.

A week ago, he might have been interested, but not today. Today, he considered himself married to a cherished woman who as much as he tried to stop, was gaining access to his heart.

Cal and he walked to the bar where a big mirror reflected the room.

"What can I do for you, gentlemen?" the small wiry man behind the bar said.

"Do you know a Lillian Rodriquez?" Cal asked.

"Sure, she hangs out here most nights," he said, staring at them. "What about her?"

"Was she with anyone in particular last night?" Jackson asked. After watching the man, Jackson knew he wasn't being honest with them. Though they had not asked the question, he was positive that Lillian was a whore and probably split the profits with George.

"Not that I remember. She did say she was meeting someone later," he said. "She left here about ten o'clock. Again, why?"

"She's dead," Jackson said.

The man's face went white and he sagged, stopped wiping down the glasses behind the bar. "We were friends."

"Her body was found not too far outside of the city limits."

He covered his face with his hands and bawled like a baby. Like the woman had meant something to him.

"She didn't deserve to die that way," he said his face red with sorrow and anger.

"No, she didn't," Cal said. "And no one was with her last night?"

"No, she drank at the bar by herself. She talked to the regulars and that was all."

"You said earlier that she was meeting someone later. Did she mention a name?"

"No, she just said he told her he needed to talk to someone, that he had been betrayed. So she left about nine o'clock last night. Told me she would see me tomorrow."

Betrayed? The only person he knew in town that had been betrayed was Lester.

Shaking his head, he said, "Who would do this?"

"We don't know, Mr. Martin, but we're Texas Rangers and we're going to find out. Do you know where Randal Jones lives?"

He gave a snort. "No, but he's playing poker at one of the tables."

Jackson glanced at the man. They needed to talk to him, see if he remembered what Lester said about Bella. It would be hard to talk and not beat the piss out of him, but he was determined to keep his emotions under control.

"Thank you, Mr. Martin. We'll let you know if we hear anything else," Cal said and with a glance at Jackson, they walked toward the poker table.

Randal saw them coming and frowned. "I'm folding. I'm sure these men are here to speak to me."

He slid his chair back and stood. "Gentlemen, are we doing this inside or outside."

The man almost acted like he thought they were going to fight him and they just needed to learn from him what Lester said about Bella. Unless he had more to offer them. Anything on who might have talked with Lillian last night or any of the other murders.

"There's a table over there," Jackson said. "We can talk there."

The three men wandered over and sank at the table. A barmaid asked what they needed and Randal ordered a beer.

"What do you want?"

"Tell us what Lester said about Bella the morning of the wedding," Jackson demanded.

The man shook his head like it was not a big deal while he repeated almost everything that Bella had told them.

"Look it was no big deal. He didn't mean it," Randal said. "His plan was to take her inheritance. Not kill her."

Jackson wasn't so certain. He wondered if they would have been investigating Bella's body if she had not run away from a disastrous marriage.

"Did you know Lillian Rodriquez?"

"Sure, she's here almost every night." He leaned in close. "Frankly, I think she was selling herself. But I wasn't going to fuck that old hag."

"She's dead," Cal told him.

It was all Jackson could do to look at the man. He was disrespectful just like his friend, Lester.

"No," the man said not certain he believed Cal. "Who would kill her?"

"That's what we're trying to find out," Cal said.

"Who *would* you fuck?" Jackson said the words and then regretted them.

"Bella Walker. Lester thought her ugly. She's a little on the plump side, but beautiful," he said.

Cal leaned across the table and grabbed the man's

shirt. "She's my wife. Don't even think about it unless you wish to die."

The man's mouth dropped open. "Lester didn't tell me."

"Was Lester here last night?" Jackson asked.

"No, he had to work at the cafe until late, so he didn't come by. Besides, he's a lousy poker player."

Jackson stood, he was ready to get out of this seedy saloon. They had spoken with the owner and also Randal. They were not any closer to learning who was doing the killing.

"Let's go," Jackson said.

Cal stood. "If you want to live, don't come near my wife."

As they walked out the door, Jackson felt a shiver run down his spine. "Do you think the killer is Randal?"

"No, the man doesn't have the spine to murder someone. I don't know who our killer is, but I'm damn ready to go home and see my bride. It's been a long day."

As they stepped out of the saloon, the sun was setting, creating an array of orange hues. Yes, Jackson was ready to go home and let Bella make them forget about what they had seen today. This part of being a Ranger he never liked.

"Let's go home," Cal said.

"I'm with you," Jackson agreed.

Climbing up on their horses, they rode down Main Street. Suddenly a young man came running toward them.

"Rangers, I got a telegram for you. Said it was urgent."

The young man handed the piece of paper up to Cal. He read it out loud. "Lester Clark wanted for the murder of his wife Jane."

Cal glanced at Jackson. "Lester must be our man. Let's get home."

20

That afternoon, Bella decided to move them from her bedroom to the downstairs one that her parents used to occupy. It was larger and would give them more space. Especially in the bed.

Her husbands would have their own dressers and until they decided on their future, everyone would be more comfortable.

The housekeeper was still away and she enjoyed organizing her husbands' things. Being married to two men was challenging and exciting and more than she'd ever dreamed of.

Right now, her life felt almost perfect. The only thing that would make it better was if she learned she was expecting. But hopefully soon.

As she carried things down the stairs, she heard someone at the door. Dropping the items on the bed, she went to answer the knock. But they told her not to open the door.

Still, she went to see who could be out there. There was no one. She glanced up and down the street and didn't see anyone.

A wrapped gift laid on the steps and she opened the door, to retrieve the package. It was probably a wedding gift from one of her friends or neighbors.

As she bent to pick it up, Lester sprang out from behind some bushes at her and she turned to flee, but he grabbed her arm. She pulled away and ran into the house but didn't have time to shut the door. If she could reach the back door, she would slip out and run for help.

Footsteps behind her alerted her he was close.

"What do you want?" she screamed. As she ran, she pulled down chairs, anything to slow him down, making a complete mess of the house, but at least her husbands would know she fought him.

"No woman ever makes me look like a fool and you made me a laughingstock in this town. You're just like the other women. And you're going to die just like them."

Fear seized her lungs. He *was* the killer. Picking up her skirts she ran like her life depended on it, because it did. She didn't know when her husbands would be back.

How could she stop him? Sprinting to the back of the house, she screamed, "Cal."

Maybe Lester would think her man was at home. But he just laughed.

"Nice try, but they're out looking at Lillian Rodriquez body. Seems she met with an accident. The same kind of accident you're going to experience."

Terror raced through her body and she ran as fast as

her short legs would carry her. When she reached the back door, she realized it was locked.

Screaming she tugged at it, but before she could open the door, he caught up with her. Whirling her around, she saw his fist come at her face. And then everything went black.

21

When Cal walked into the house, his body went cold as he stared at the strewn mess of chairs. Slowly he and Jackson searched through the house. When they reached the back door, there was blood on the floor.

"She was doing her best to get away," Jackson said his voice deep and low and Cal knew deadly.

"Let's go," Cal said. "I've seen enough. He's taken her."

"Wait. It's dark, let's think about this. All the other women have been found in ditches. He's going to want to kill her and then leave town, because he knows we're onto him."

They glanced at one another.

"Remember Bella said he wanted to go to the Black Hills of North Dakota. I think he'll be headed there. Let's take the road that goes north. That's the quickest, and God willing, we'll find him there. But we don't have long. He'll kill her to spite us," Cal said.

They ran out the door and jumped on their horses.

They didn't have time to stop and tell the sheriff. Cal's focus was on finding Bella. And if Lester wasn't on the road to North Dakota, they would lose Bella, and Cal wasn't certain he could live knowing they had lost her to an evil man.

As they rode out of town, he noticed that the cafe had a for sale sign in the window. Yes, Lester was leaving town and for gold hunting.

It was getting dark as they rode out. Pitch black, and for once, Cal was glad there was no bright moon. Because he would light a fire and they would be able to see it, the closer they came.

Two hours later, Cal saw the small glow of a campfire and sent up a prayer that it was them.

"Look," Cal said.

"You confront Lester and I'll sneak up from the back," Jackson said.

They tied their horses far enough away that Lester would not hear them and then stealthily made their way toward the camp.

The sight the campfire revealed made Cal want to rush into their camp, his heart pounded in his chest as rage filled him. Bella's wrists were tied to a tree limb. Methodically, Lester was stripping her clothes off or slashing them with the knife.

The man intended to rape her before he killed her. They had gotten here just in time. Cal would give Jackson time to set up, but he'd rush the camp before Lester could fulfill his plan.

"Your husband is going to find you naked, tied in the

tree with my seed dried on your legs."

A rag was stuffed in her mouth and tears flowed down her cheeks. He laid the knife's blade against her face. "Maybe I'll carve my initials in your face. That way there won't be any doubt about who killed you."

He took the knife and ran it down her side, cutting her chemise, but also leaving behind a small trickle of blood.

"But first I'm going to torture you. Then I'll enjoy your sweet flesh before I end your life."

The man was a sadist, enjoying hurting women. Completely sick.

Cal couldn't wait any longer. He pulled out his Colt and burst into the camp. "Drop the knife."

Lester jumped behind Bella, putting her body between him and Cal. "Where's Jackson? Usually where there is one of you the second one is not far away."

"Have I told you that he's a sharp shooter? He's the best shot in the Texas Rangers."

Lester looked around nervously.

"If you surrender, you could be spared."

"For how long? No, they would hang me."

He put the knife up next to Bella's throat and her eyes widened with terror.

"Besides, she's going to die. There is nothing you can do to stop me. If I go, so does Bella," he said with a laugh. "This bitch is worse than all the others. Even my first wife didn't humiliate me as bad as this one."

Cal knew he had to keep Lester talking until Jackson had a good sight on him. It was all he could do to keep from rushing the man, but he feared that knife would find its way into Bella.

"How many women have you killed?"

Lester grinned and shrugged. "Not enough. Stupid bitches always betray you. From my mother to my first wife and especially Bella. She has to die."

He drew back the blade to end her life and Cal was certain he was going to kill her. The man hated Bella.

"Now you're going to get to witness my handiwork with the knife," he said with a grin that made Cal's blood freeze in his veins.

"And when that knife hits her neck, my bullet will enter your brain," Cal said, raising his gun.

The man laughed. "I'll be dead. No trial or hanging for me. And your wife will also be dead. Neither one of us will have her."

Cal wanted to charge the man but knew that would only get Bella killed. He raised his gun, when suddenly the boom of a weapon sounded behind Lester and a hole opened in his brain as he slumped to the ground. The knife falling from his hand.

Jackson.

Bella was screaming inside the rag stuffed in her mouth. Tears streamed down her face and Cal rushed to her side. Taking out his pocket knife, he sliced through the ropes around her wrist that had her hung from a limb.

She fell into his arms, sobbing.

"Bella, it's over. He's dead," Cal said, holding onto his wife like he would never let her go. If they had come any later, they would have been too late.

His wife hysterical, he held her trembling body until Jackson, too, wrapped his arms around her. They held her between them as her body shook with nerves.

"I was so afraid. I didn't think you'd find me before he killed me," she sobbed. "And then when the bullet hit his brain."

She cried harder.

"I'm sorry, honey, but if I didn't kill him, he was going to kill you," Jackson said. "That was the only way I could shoot him."

She nodded. "I know, but I thought I'd been shot."

They held her between them until she calmed down.

"Thank you," she said. "I didn't let him in. He tricked me."

"We know," Jackson said. "Thank goodness you said he wanted to go to the Black Hills of North Dakota. That's the only reason we found you."

"Can we please go home," she said with a sob. "I want to lie in bed between my husbands."

"Agreed," Cal said. "The sooner the better."

While Jackson held her, Cal went to their horses. When he returned, they wrapped her in a blanket and took her home.

22

The next two days, Jackson walked around unable to shake how close they had come to losing Bella. Since they brought her home, they had coddled her, held her, loved her, but had not fucked her.

Even now, he feared touching her because if he continued on this path, she would have his heart and soul. And then he would be so vulnerable. Lester's kidnapping had showed him that he was well on his way to being exposed.

And every time he looked at her, his heart clenched with terror and his dick would hardened. All he could do was think about Bella. All he could do was dream about the next time they took her.

Part of him wanted to run out the door, jump on his horse, and ride away and then Cal would give him that look that recognized that Jackson was dealing with his demons.

Demons that haunted him. Last night, he had suffered

a nightmare. Bella had awakened him and held him close the rest of the night. Feeling her comforting arms had almost been his undoing.

Yet, just her touch calmed him.

After her ordeal, it was his job to comfort her and yet she had comforted him.

Tonight, he and Cal planned to claim her together and yet he wasn't certain he could take that final step. Oh, he wanted to, but if he did, she would own him, body and soul. Then if something did happen to her, he wouldn't be able to live.

With a sigh, he glanced at the woman his heart would claim tonight. Could he make that final commitment?

"Gentlemen, I'll be waiting in the bedroom, naked," she said.

It was the first time since the kidnapping that she showed any interest in having sex and Cal's eyes grew large. "We'll be in there in five minutes."

A sense of fear came over Jackson.

"You going to be all right?" Cal asked. "You haven't been yourself since Lester took our wife."

"I swore I would never love anyone again and I'm falling so hard, it's crazy."

Cal gave a chuckle. "Me too."

"Why would it hurt for you to love again?" Cal asked. "They didn't die because of your lack of responsibility."

It was the first time his brother questioned his decision and that stunned him.

"I can't risk losing her. What if next time I don't kill the man before he kills her. What if she dies in childbirth? What if I come home one day and she's dead?"

Cal sighed and clapped him on the back.

"I'm not going to lie to you, it would hurt. It would be devastating. But I'm going to live for today, for the moment and enjoy the time we have together. Instead of concentrating on how it would feel if something happens to her, I'm going to love her with all my heart and soul until I take my last breath here on earth or she takes hers."

Was he concentrating on the negative? But walking into his home and finding his entire family killed, devastated him. For weeks, he couldn't move. Couldn't think as the grief rode him hard.

Was it time to let it go?

"I don't know," he said.

"She knows something's wrong and she doesn't understand," Cal said. "You need to talk to her."

Very few people knew what happened to his family. Only his closest friends and that was only Cal.

Cal stood and Jackson followed him into the bedroom.

She sat naked on the bed. "First, I want to talk."

The men sank down on the bed beside her.

She licked her lips as tears filled her eyes. "First, I want to tell you thank you for rescuing me the other night. What we have together is so special and all I could think about was that I would never experience being in your arms again. I would never have your children."

Cal wrapped an arm around her. "It's all right. That's our job as your husbands."

"The other thing I want to talk about is you, Jackson.

Since that night, you've been distant. You've had nightmares." She reached up and caressed the side of his face. "I love you. I love both of you. You each have a special place in my heart."

Jackson knew this was his moment to tell her everything, but he didn't like talking about the subject and they had suffered something near tragic this week.

Cal, leaned over and kissed her soundly on the lips. "Bella, I love you so much. The first day we rescued you is the best day of my life."

She caressed Cal's face. "Me too."

Jackson knew Cal had told her about his wife and how she died from a snakebite. But he wasn't certain he was ready to tell her about his family. Because if he admitted his feelings for them, he would also be admitting his feelings for her.

Suddenly she faced Jackson. "Since the day Lester kidnapped me, you've not been my demanding man. Help me understand. I'm your wife and I love you. Talk to me and tell me what's bothering you."

Her big blue eyes stared at him with the softest expression, shining with pure love. How could he not tell her? How could he deny himself the pleasure she offered him?

Was it time for him to let himself love again?

A heavy sigh escaped him. "Five years ago, I left home to train with the Texas Rangers. My mother was so proud of me. When I completed my training my family planned a big party with my younger brothers and sisters. When I arrived home, I found everyone shot and killed. A rogue band of Indians came through and killed my family."

He started to shake at the memory of riding up to the house and seeing his father lying on the porch, dead.

Bella wrapped her arms around him and held him close.

"My mother, my sister Stella, Jim, Joe, and my father were all killed. After I buried them, I couldn't eat, sleep, or do anything as grief overcame me. The pain was so bad, that I swore I would never give my heart to anyone ever again. Because the loss is just too much."

"And then Lester kidnapped me and brought back all those feelings," she said quietly.

"Yes, I...I want to love you, but I'm afraid. Terrified," he said in a whisper.

"This is why you had the nightmare the other night," she said in a soothing voice.

"Yes."

With a sigh, she gazed into his eyes, giving him her heart.

"What can I do to make it easier for you? You don't have to love me if you're afraid. You don't have to be my husband, though it would hurt terribly if you left us. But I want you to be happy. You will always have my heart and soul, my love. I'll wait for you as long as it takes," she told him.

The woman was giving him the moon and the stars and heavens. She was doing her best to make him comfortable with loving her.

With a deep sigh, he turned to her. "Know that I love you. Know that you have captured my heart and made me whole again, but sometimes I may grow frightened. And please, dear God, never leave me," he said in a husky whisper, tears filling his eyes as he stared at the woman who had seized his heart though he'd done everything he could not to love her.

She reached up and brought his lips down to hers and kissed him in a tender way that let him know he'd be crazy to walk away from her love.

"I give you my word that if I'm taken from this earth, it won't be because I wanted to go." She grabbed Cal's hand and looked between the two of them. "Our marriage is unusual, it's different from most, but I'm the happiest I've ever been in my life. Now will one of you, please fuck me."

The two men laughed, stood, and shed their clothes.

Bella crawled up on the bed and took the position with her forehead on the bed, her ass in the air.

"Tonight we're going to claim you at the same time. You're ready." Cal told her.

"Will it hurt?"

"If it does, you tell us. We're not doing our job properly," Jackson told her, knowing he wanted to make this the best sex she had ever experienced in her life. This woman understood him and he couldn't ask for anything more.

Cal slid beneath her, his lips covering hers, possessing her.

With her ass in the air, Jackson's fingers rolled her clit, twisting the little nub of nerves. A groan filled the air and she pushed her ass back.

With a *thunk* on the end of the butt plug, he began to twist it, pulling it almost out and then putting it back in.

She gasped as he assaulted her clit and her puckered rosebud all at once.

Finally, she broke the kiss and glanced back at him over her shoulder. "I'm yours, Jackson Moore, take me. And you too, Cal. You are my men, make me yours."

Cal lined up his cock at her pussy opening, his fingers spreading her wide. "I'm going to shove my cock in you as far as it will go."

"Oh, please do," she groaned.

"And then I'm going to take your ass," Jackson said as he grabbed a jar of lotion and rubbed it on his cock and around her little rosebud. He pulled the plug completely out, knowing they would never need it again.

Knowing that soon, they would share her in every way possible.

Impatiently he waited for Cal as he pushed his cock into her sweet pussy. As soon as he was fully inside, Jackson pressed his cock at her ass. She turned and glanced at him over her shoulder.

"Fuck me, Jackson," she cried. "Fuck me."

Slowly his cock entered her. The walls squeezing him, resisting him.

He slapped her ass. "Relax, Bella. Let me in."

"I'm trying," she said. "But you're filling me up. The two of you are stretching me so wide. And it feels so good."

"Just a little more," he told her, knowing that once he was in, she would be theirs. He felt her rectum stretch, his cock suddenly plunging in.

"Aargh," she cried.

For a moment, he didn't move as he gave her time to

adjust to the feeling of the fullness. He loved the way the walls clenched around his cock.

Then he felt Cal begin to move and he also moved inside her. As one pulled out, the other shoved in. Soon they had a rhythm going and he could feel his seed building. No, he wasn't ready for this to end.

They had waited so long to experience her together and as much as he tried, he was not going to last long.

Reaching between her legs, he found her clit and pushed it against Cal's cock and she groaned.

"Baby, I'm not going to last much longer. Come whenever you're ready, because I'm about to coat your pussy walls with my seed."

Jackson knew that he wouldn't last much longer either. With his hand, he slapped her cheeks once more and this time she screamed as her orgasm tore through her. It was like an avalanche as they all three came at the same time.

Together. The three of them, as it was meant to be.

As his seed spilled into her rectum, his heart overflowed with love for this woman and he knew he would never be the same. Finally, he had put the past behind him and his future was with Bella and Cal.

They all three collapsed on the bed, their bodies entwined as they slowly returned to earth. Never had he experienced such a great night of sex. Never.

When finally his heart had slowed and his lungs were functioning, he pulled Bella into his arms. "Your love has healed me and made me whole again. I love you, Bella."

"And I love you," Cal said.

"You are my men. My husbands. My life. My loves."

23

Three Years Later

From the kitchen window, Bella watched Cal chase their son, Michael, around the yard. Today he was eighteen months old and he loved to be outdoors. She smiled as his big emerald eyes with dark lashes danced with merriment.

They never talked about whose child he was, but she felt certain that he was Jackson's. And the next baby, she hoped would be Cal's.

She had yet to tell her men she was expecting, but she felt certain the next babe was growing in her belly.

It was hard to believe they had been married for three years. After they finished Lester's investigation, both men had resigned from the Texas Rangers and they all moved to Cal's ranch in East Texas.

Leaving Blessing, her home, her friends had been hard, but she would follow her men to the ends of the earth to be near them.

Her horse Midnight had already produced two beautiful mares and they hoped that soon he would produce a stallion. The beautiful horse enjoyed the countryside and even let Cal ride him.

But more than anything, they were happy. Not a day went by that Bella didn't thank the good Lord for her husbands and for saving her from Lester. She never expected this marriage to be so fulfilling and it couldn't be better.

She walked outside to where Jackson watched Cal chase their son around the yard.

"You all right?" he asked as he glanced up at her worry in his emerald eyes. Oh, how she loved this man and with every little ache or pain she had, he was right there concerned.

She'd been sick this morning and that's why she was certain she was pregnant again. Morning sickness like before and her breasts were so tender, she didn't want her men to touch them, which was hard for them.

"Feeling better," she said.

"What do you think was wrong," Jackson asked his eyes suddenly gleaming.

"Morning sickness. Looks like babe number two is growing inside me."

Cal stopped and glanced at her. "Really?"

She smiled. "Yes, really."

Her men came to her side and wrapped their arms around her.

"Thank you," Cal said. "I can't wait."

"Me too, love," Jackson said. "May the good Lord watch

over you and our babe."

She loved that Jackson was now able to call her *love* and tell her how much he loved her. He still occasionally had nightmares, but overall, he had put his family's deaths behind him.

"Maybe this one will be a girl," she said, loving her men. "I love both of you and our little family."

"Me too," Cal said.

"Yes," Jackson replied. "Our family."

"Thank God, I became a runaway bride who ran straight into my two cowboys."

They all smiled as they watched their son, now chasing a butterfly. Life was good.

※

THANK YOU SO MUCH READING. I enjoyed writing this story because of the western serial killer angle. I hope you enjoyed Bella finding happiness. Next up Two Cowboys Too Perfect. Here is a sneak peak!

※

ELLA DILLARD OPENED the front door of her home on the edge of Blessing, Texas. On this bright beautiful spring morning, six riders sat staring at her house. Fear scurried down her spine and settled in her core as she gazed at the rugged men.

Half a dozen riders who looked meaner than a hungry spring rattler ready to pounce.

"Morning, ma'am," a man with a black hat pulled low over his eyes called. "We're waiting on Richard. Have you seen him?"

Her brother. What the hell did these men want with her eighteen-year-old brother? Since their parents' unexpected death, he'd lost his way and no matter what she did, nothing seemed to help him.

And now these men, who looked like a gang of outlaws, were waiting on him.

"Just a minute," she said and closed the door, locking it behind her. She hurried up the stairs to Richard's room. He walked out just as she reached the landing.

"There are some rough looking characters waiting outside for you. Who are they?"

He ignored her and hurried down the stairs.

"Richard, I said who are these men?" she asked again, following behind him.

"None of your business. I've got to go," he said, unlocking and then yanking open the front door, not bothering to close it.

She hurried out after him. They had a horse saddled and ready for him.

"About time you showed up," the one man said to him. "Who's this?"

"My sister," he said, climbing up on the horse. "Let's go."

"Where are you going?" she asked, standing on the porch.

Ignoring her, he turned his horse and kicked the mare's side to ride away, leaving her questions unanswered.

The unnerving looking guy grinned at her and she noticed that part of his ear lobe was missing. "Don't worry. We'll have him home before dark." He winked at her. "It would be real nice if you had dinner waiting on us."

A tremor of unease scurried down her spine. Where were they going? For some reason, she didn't feel easy about these men. They wore the look of someone who thought nothing of killing.

Life didn't matter to them.

In stunned disbelief, she watched them ride away. What had her brother gotten himself involved with now?

They looked like a gang of vicious outlaws, but how could she know? She had to go to the sheriff. Maybe he would know what to do. Maybe he could help her stop her brother from getting involved with them.

Maybe Richard would listen to another man.

Why did she have a feeling that already he was riding with them but for what reason? They all knew him by name. They were waiting for him.

After they rode off, she locked the house and began to walk the ten blocks to town. When her parents died in a carriage accident, she had inherited the house and raising her brother. At the time, she had just turned eighteen and Richard was only fifteen. But now he was old enough to make his own decisions. Now he was determined to become a legend.

And so far, he had not made wise choices regarding his life.

With a sigh, she hurried toward the law office before she went to school to teach her class. Her students would be waiting and yet she had other things that were pressing that she must take care of first.

Her boots sounded sharp against the wooden sidewalk outside the lawman's office. When she opened the door, two men were inside talking to the sheriff, Seth Ingram.

The space was a typical small-town sheriff's office with a desk, cabinets, Wanted posters on the wall and a two-cell jail – one she feared her brother would soon be looking through the bars of.

"Good morning, Miss Dillard," Seth said with concern on his face. "Is there something you need?"

Wringing her hands, she walked inside. "Sheriff, maybe it's nothing, but this morning my brother, Richard, rode off with a group of men that, frankly, frightened me. He wouldn't tell me anything about them. You know he's been getting into so much trouble lately. I'm afraid he's joined some kind of terrifying gang."

One of the seated men stood. "Here, have a seat. Warren Alley, Texas Ranger, and this is my friend, Clinton Flowers, Texas Ranger."

"Thank you," she said. Warren's handsome looks caused her heart to beat a little faster. Dark hair and the largest brown eyes she'd ever seen were covered by long, thick eyelashes that hid his expressive gaze. "Ella Dillard."

"Miss Dillard, can you describe these men to us? We're searching for the Evans gang, a group of men who like to rob stagecoaches and banks in their spare time. They've killed at least two men."

Could this be the same gang the rangers were searching for?

"How would my brother have met them? No, it just can't be who he's involved with."

And yet, she was so afraid her brother had found trouble.

"Did one of the men have an ear lobe missing the bottom." A sizzle of fear traveled from her neck all the way to her knees causing them to shake when the men nodded.

"How many men were there?" Warren asked her, coming to sit on the sheriff's desk right in front of her.

"Six and my brother made seven. He wouldn't tell me where they were going."

Clinton glanced at the sheriff. "When's the next gold shipment for the bank?"

"Today," he replied. "Should come in about noon."

She glanced at her pin watch. "I need to get to school. The students are waiting for me."

All this talk of gangs, gold, and bank robberies was making her nervous. What if Richard was involved? What if he were shot and killed? He was the last of her family. As much as she hated what he was doing, she still loved him.

Warren picked up some Wanted posters lying on a credenza and brought them back.

"Take a look at these and let me know if you recognize any of these men," he said.

With her heart pattering in her chest like a locomotive, she glanced at the images. Of the six he had, several were of men she saw at her house this morning.

"These four were there. They're coming back tonight, promising they would have Richard home before dark. What do I do if they come back to my house?"

What was her brother thinking? Didn't he realize that men like these would think nothing of harming them to get whatever it was they wanted?

"What time are you done teaching school?"

"About three o'clock."

"We're going to meet the stage and ride in with them," Clinton said. "We should be back about three. We'll escort you home and wait with you for your brother and his friends to return."

She bit her bottom lip, nerves causing her stomach to flutter. It wasn't that she didn't want them at her house, she really did, but somehow, she had to protect her sibling.

"You're not going to arrest my brother, are you?"

"As long as he hasn't done anything too stupid. We'd like to talk with him, but more than anything, we want to catch the Daniel Evans gang. They're ruthless killers," Warren said.

"Go enjoy teaching school. This afternoon, we'll follow you home," Clinton assured her.

Ella stood and glanced at the two men. They were Texas Rangers; they had stars on their chests that proclaimed who they were. But they were also big, strong, handsome men that she would have enjoyed the feel of their arms around her protecting her.

When she glanced into their eyes, she wanted to touch their square jaws. Feel the texture of their skin. Smell the husky man scent.

And tonight, they were coming to her home. Did she have something she could cook for them? And were they married? There were no rings on their fingers.

What was she thinking? They were strangers and would soon be gone from Blessing.

The image of her brother came to mind. "I just hope Richard is not stupid enough to get involved with these men. I don't want to see my only living relative hang."

"We'll do our best, ma'am, to get him on the right path," Clinton promised. "Now, may I escort you to the school?"

She smiled. "Yes, thank you. It's about two blocks from here."

He took her elbow and led her out the door. A rush of warmth filled her at the commanding feel of his fingers on her bare skin.

No man had intrigued her like these two and yet she only needed one.

Click here to continue reading!

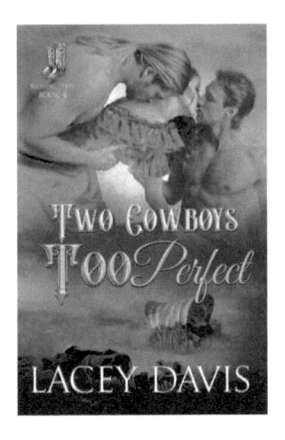

PLEASE LEAVE A REVIEW

Did you enjoy the book? Reviews help authors. I would appreciate you posting a review. Click here to leave a review.

Follow Lacey Davis on Facebook.

Sign up for my New Book Alert and receive a free book.

Also By Lacey Davis

Blessing, Texas Series
Loving My Cowboys
Two Cowboys' Christmas Bride
Two Cowboys One Bride
Two Cowboys Too Perfect
Two Cowboys to Protect Her
Two Cowboys Save Christmas — November 2021

Bridgewater Brides World
Their Perfect Bride
Their Tempting Bride
Their Scandalous Bride—October 2021

Want to learn about my new releases before anyone else? Sign up for my New Book Alert and receive a complimentary book. Blindfold Me.

ABOUT THE AUTHOR

Lacey Davis is a pseudonym for a USA Today bestselling author who wanted to try her hand at writing sexy romance. With these novels, I hope to write sizzling romances that will leave you grabbing a fan to cool yourself off.

If you like hunky bad boy heroes who like to be in charge and strong pretty women who are willing to risk it all, then look no further. These sexy reads will get you in the mood. Come experience strong women who will tame these bad boys and leave them wanting more.

The End

Made in United States
Troutdale, OR
07/14/2023